replica

The Best
of the Best

MARILYN KAYE

BANTAM BOOKS
NEW YORK • TORONTO • LONDON • SYDNEY • AUCKLAND

RL 5.5, 008–012
THE BEST OF THE BEST
A Bantam Skylark Book / September 1999

For information address: Bantam Doubleday Dell Books for Young Readers.

ISBN 0-553-48687-X

Published simultaneously in the United States and Canada.

Bantam Books are published by Bantam Books, a division of Random House, Inc. Its trademark, consisting of the words "Bantam Books" and the portrayal of a rooster, is Registered in U.S. Patent and Trademark Office and in other countries. Marca Registrada. Bantam Books, 1540 Broadway, New York, New York 10036.

PRINTED IN THE UNITED STATES OF AMERICA

OPM   0   9   8   7   6   5   4   3   2   1

For Marie-Hélène Polloni, Vincent Soulier, Raphaël, and Maxim, with love and gratitude for helping to make Paris a second home for me

The Best
of the Best

one

At the table in the Morgans' dining room, Amy and Tasha faced each other over a Scrabble board. "What time is it?" Tasha asked.

"You asked me that two minutes ago," Amy replied. "It was four-twenty-nine then. It is now four-thirty-one." She removed three Scrabble tiles from her rack and arranged them on the board. Using the *j* from Tasha's last word, *jealousy,* she added a *u,* an *m,* and a *p.* "Double letter score under the *p,*" she murmured, and noted her total on the pad of paper by her side. Then she took three new letter tiles from the bag.

Tasha took a moment to examine her own selection

of letters. Then, using the *p* from Amy's *jump,* she added all of her seven tiles to the board. *"Pathetic,"* she declared. "Let's see, that makes . . ." She began to calculate her points.

It wasn't necessary. Amy had already done the math in her head, and she knew that Tasha now had a score three times her own. She mentally berated herself for not having glanced through a dictionary before agreeing to this game. Examining the possibilities for her next move, she saw nothing but gibberish in her letters. She was grateful when Eric came bounding into the room and interrupted them.

"What time is it?" he asked.

Amy looked at her watch for the zillionth time. "Four-thirty-four," she replied. "No, it's four-thirty-five. And before either of you asks me again, I can tell you right now that in precisely one minute it will be four-thirty-six."

Eric sighed. "I'm bored. Man, I hate these No-TV Weeks. I mean, what's the point?"

"The point," Amy said, "according to the school board, is to encourage us to do something more meaningful and intelligent with our time."

"Amy, take your turn," Tasha ordered.

Amy put a *c* and an *a* in the spaces above Tasha's *t.* *"Cat,"* she said.

"Very intelligent." Eric smiled. "Almost brilliant."

Amy made a face at him. "I'd like to see you do any better with these letters."

Eric moved around the table to look at the letters Tasha was holding. "Tasha's in worse shape than you are," he told Amy. "What's she going to do with an *x* when she doesn't have an *r*, *a*, and *y*?"

"*X-ray* isn't the only word that contains an *x*," Tasha said. With that, she used an available *e* on the board and added *xplicit*. Once again, she'd managed to use up all her tiles and add substantially to her tally.

Amy was impressed. "There's no way I'm going to beat you."

"I know," Tasha said smugly. "It's kind of nice knowing there's still something I can do better than you."

Amy grinned. She knew that Tasha knew that if Amy *really* cared about winning, she could memorize the pages of a dictionary and beat anyone at Scrabble. But it was more fun to play as if she were a regular person.

"Amy," Tasha said, "what—"

"Four-forty-one," Amy answered before Tasha finished the question.

"You can read minds now too?" Eric asked.

"No, just a lucky guess." Amy looked at her watch again. "Wow, now it's four-forty-two! Time flies, huh? Only eighteen minutes till five o'clock."

3

Tasha frowned. "Do you really think it's okay for us to turn on the TV at five?"

"I think we can make an exception in this case," Amy reassured her. "After all, it's not every day that our very own school gets to be on the news."

"Besides," Eric added, "it's not like the TV police are going to show up and arrest us."

"But we *did* sign that no-TV contract," Tasha reminded them.

Tasha was very big on ethics. That was one of the many qualities Amy loved in her best friend. So she tried to think of a way to ease Tasha's mind.

"Wait," she said. "Didn't that contract say something like 'I will not watch TV for a week'? *Watch* TV. It didn't say anything about not listening to it."

Tasha brightened. "Good point!"

"You're both nuts," Eric stated, and left the dining room.

"Did you see him today?" Tasha asked Amy.

She didn't need to explain whom she was referring to. For weeks, Amy and everyone else had been talking about the new student who would be attending Parkside Middle School, and who had shown up for the first time that very day.

"No, but I saw the TV woman. Kids were going nuts.

You know Alan Greenfield? He was following the reporter, and every time the camera lights went on he jumped in front of the camera and waved."

Tasha shuddered. "I hope *that's* not on TV. People will think we're a school for clowns. Did you get a lecture in homeroom?"

Amy nodded. "Yeah, I think everyone did. 'Don't stare, don't point, treat the new kid like everyone else.' . . . Personally, I don't think that's going to be possible. Everyone's too excited."

From the living room, they heard the click of the TV coming on. "Let's stay in the dining room so we won't be tempted to look," Tasha suggested. "Eric! Turn it up louder so we can hear it in here!"

Naturally, the situation at Parkside wasn't considered a big story. First they had to sit through a lot of other stuff—the mayor said this, the police chief said that. A shooting, a mugging, a drug bust—standard Los Angeles news. Amy's own suburban neighborhood was rarely mentioned, thank goodness.

Finally, twenty-five minutes into the newscast, the story they were waiting for was introduced.

"Ordinarily, the arrival of a new student at Parkside Middle School wouldn't be a media event," the newswoman said in a chirpy voice. "But the student arriving this morning isn't any ordinary student. Today Adrian Peele begins the ninth grade here at Parkside. What's so strange about that? you may ask. Well, Adrian Peele is just eight years old. He has been promoted from the second grade to the ninth grade. According to school officials, little Adrian is a child prodigy, a certified genius."

It was hard for Amy to stay in the dining room, knowing that by now a picture of the genius was probably on the screen. She was dying to see what he looked like.

"Adrian, how do you like your new school?" the chirpy woman was asking.

The voice that responded was definitely childlike. But the words weren't childish at all. "It's difficult to say at this point in time, and it would be premature to base my assessment on early impressions. Excuse me, I don't want to be late for my class."

"Well, it appears that Adrian is very serious about his education! Let's talk to some other students at Parkside and get their reactions to the presence of a real-life prodigy in their midst. What's your name?"

"Jeanine Bryant."

Amy and Tasha exchanged looks. Of course Jeanine would find some way to get herself on TV. She never passed up the chance for attention.

"Jeanine, how do you feel about having a genius attending school with you?"

Artificial enthusiasm and warmth practically oozed from Jeanine's mouth. "I'm just so proud that Adrian's family has selected Parkside. And I'm going to do my best to make sure Adrian feels welcome and comfortable here. I'm only in seventh grade, but I want to be his friend."

Amy groaned. "Poor kid. Maybe we should warn him." Jeanine was her least favorite classmate at Parkside. She was a stuck-up, know-it-all, conceited snob who'd been competing with Amy for every possible honor since kindergarten.

The chirpy-voiced reporter was speaking again. "And this young man is ninth-grader Eric Morgan."

All ethical concerns about watching TV vanished. Amy and Tasha raced into the living room. Sure enough, there on the screen was the face of Tasha's brother and Amy's boyfriend.

"Eric, I understand that you have a special relationship with Adrian."

It was very clear that Eric wasn't as eager for media attention as Jeanine had been. His eyes darted back and forth, as if he was looking for a way to escape. "Uh, yeah, I guess. Dr. Noble, that's our principal, she asked me to be Adrian's big brother. I'm going to show him around and stuff."

"How do you feel about this?"

"Fine."

"Thank you, Eric. Let's go back to the newsroom now."

"Eric!" Tasha cried out. "Why didn't you tell us?"

Eric gave the girls an abashed grin. "Surprise."

"What's he like?" Amy asked.

"Yeah, did he exude genius rays?" Tasha wanted to know.

Eric held up one of his hands. "Please. I only met him for two seconds. I'll get back to you."

Amy sat on the arm of Eric's chair and put her arm around his shoulders. "I'm glad you'll be helping him out. I know he's supposed to be supersmart, but he's still a little kid. It won't be easy for him, being so different. I know. Eric, he's lucky to have someone like you watching out for him."

Eric reddened. Compliments embarrassed him. "Yeah, well, whatever," he mumbled as he got up and went to the window.

"I just had a brilliant idea," Tasha said suddenly. "You know how I'm a junior reporter for the *Journal*? Wouldn't an interview with Adrian Peele make a great article?"

"I thought you were already writing an article about No-TV Week," Amy said.

"But that's boring," Tasha told her. "All the schools are having these dumb No-TV Weeks, and they've been doing it for years. Having a child prodigy in your own school is much more interesting. And with Eric being his big brother, I could get close to him."

Eric groaned.

"What's the matter? You think I'm going to embarrass you or something?"

"It's not that," Eric muttered. "Someone's coming."

Amy faked a look of alarm. "Uh-oh, is it the TV police?" She picked up the remote and turned off the set.

"Worse," Eric said. "It's Jeremy Spitzer."

"Who's Jeremy Spitzer?" Tasha asked.

Eric mumbled something so garbled even Amy couldn't make out the words.

"What?" she asked.

Eric spoke through clenched teeth. "My biology tutor."

Tasha explained. "Eric got a C for his midterm grade in biology. Mom and Dad said he had to have some extra help."

"*Oh.*" Amy couldn't blame Eric for not telling her himself. It wasn't exactly the kind of thing that a person bragged about to his girlfriend. She was on the verge of telling him that *she* could have tutored him in biology—all she had to do was read the ninth-grade textbook and her photographic memory would take care of the rest.

But maybe that wasn't such a good idea. It wasn't always easy for Eric to have a girlfriend who could do everything better than he could.

She joined Eric at the window and looked at the approaching figure. "He doesn't look old enough to be a tutor," she said.

"Well, he's my age, and he's in my class," Eric said gloomily. "He's a real brainiac. My teacher asked him to help me."

"What did you say his name is?" Tasha asked. "Jerry?"

"*Jeremy,*" Eric corrected her. "And whatever you do, don't call him Jerry."

"Why not?" Amy asked, but there was no time for Eric to explain. The tutor was knocking on the front door.

She soon discovered the reason behind Eric's advice. Jeremy Spitzer wasn't the kind of guy anyone would call Jerry. Any nickname would be way too casual and friendly.

Jeremy was stiff and cold, and he had the thinnest lips Amy had ever seen. He barely acknowledged the girls when Eric introduced them, and his nose wrinkled as he gazed around the cozy living room. He looked like he was smelling something bad.

"Where are we going to work?" he asked Eric. "Your room?"

"Uh, my room's kind of a mess," Eric told him. "Clothes all over the place. Computer games covering my desk. You know how it is."

It was apparent from Jeremy's expression that he had no idea what Eric was talking about. Amy imagined that Jeremy's room had to be immaculate.

"Let's go into the dining room," Eric suggested.

"We'll clear up the Scrabble game," Tasha said. Amy followed her to the table, where they started to pick up the game pieces. Jeremy looked at the board.

"*C-a-t. Cat?*"

"Yeah, that's how it's spelled," Amy said brightly. "I guess that looks pretty simple to you, huh?"

"It would look simple to anyone over the age of six," Jeremy replied.

Amy bristled. "Well, I didn't have any good letters. It isn't enough to be intelligent to play Scrabble, you know. You have to have good luck."

Jeremy gazed at her through half-closed eyes. "I know all about Scrabble. I was the regional teen champion last year."

"Oh." He was beginning to irritate her. "So, you're a genius in biology *and* language arts. You must be a real whiz kid."

"Comparatively speaking," Jeremy said. He sat down at the table, opened his backpack, and took out books and papers.

" 'Comparatively speaking,' " Tasha repeated. "What's *that* supposed to mean?"

Eric was looking uneasy. "Hey, you two, don't pick on my tutor. I need him. He's the smartest guy in our class."

"Well, maybe that won't be so true in the future," Amy commented. "Now that Adrian Peele's here."

Jeremy looked up. "Who?" He acted as if he'd never heard the name before. Amy didn't buy it. Everyone at Parkside Middle School knew about the prodigy.

"Adrian Peele," she repeated. "The eight-year-old genius. You must be looking forward to meeting him."

"Why should I be interested in meeting *him*?"

"Well, he's someone on your level," Amy said. She couldn't resist adding, "If not higher."

A pained expression crossed Jeremy's face. "I can't imagine that I'll have anything in common with an eight-year-old freak of nature."

"Why do you think he's a freak?" Tasha asked.

"Because it's obvious that he's the result of some sort of genetic accident that has accelerated his ability to learn prematurely. There have been cases like this before, and they usually burn out at an early age. It's highly doubtful that he'll be able to sustain his ability. True prodigies are very rare." To Amy's ears, Jeremy was implying that he was one of them.

He turned to Eric. "Shall we begin? What do you know about DNA?"

"DNA?" Eric repeated. "It's something to do with genes, right?"

Jeremy let out a long, weary sigh. "Deoxyribonucleic acid. The substance that contains the genetic information for most organisms." He glanced at Tasha and Amy. "I really don't want an audience for this session. And I can't imagine either of you have any interest in or knowledge of genetics."

Amy and Tasha fled the room and ran upstairs to Tasha's bedroom. There they collapsed on one of the twin beds and doubled over in laughter.

"What a *creep*!" Tasha cried out. "Can you believe that jerk?" She mimicked Jeremy's haughty voice. " 'You girls don't know anything about genetics, do you?' "

"Oh no, nothing at all," Amy said, giggling so hard

she could barely catch her breath. "If he thinks Adrian Peele is a freak of nature, can you imagine what he'd say about me?" She hopped off the bed and struck a pose. "Allow me to introduce myself. I am Amy, Number Seven. I was conceived in a laboratory. I was cultivated from identical DNA strands made up of selected genetic material. I am physically and intellectually superior to any other human being. I am stronger, I can see farther, hear better, and I can learn more quickly than any child prodigy."

Again Tasha imitated Jeremy's tone. "I find that difficult to believe. Can you demonstrate your superior skills?"

Amy pretended to consider that. She gazed at Tasha intensely. "Jeremy . . . is that yellow wax in your ears? And a gigantic booger in your nose?"

Now Tasha was laughing hysterically, and Amy fell back onto the bed to laugh with her.

"I wonder," Tasha said when she finally got control of herself again, "what Jeremy would say if you really told him that."

"He'd think I was crazy," Amy said promptly. "Or he'd call me a liar."

"Or he could be out-of-his-mind jealous," Tasha added.

"Possibly," Amy acknowledged. Of course, pondering Jeremy's reaction was a waste of time. Because he would never know that Amy was really and truly a product of creative genetic engineering. One of twelve identical organisms. And an honest-to-goodness clone.

t w o

2

One week later, Eric sat in the small reception area outside the principal's office at Parkside. He waited alongside two frightened seventh-graders who had been caught scribbling graffiti on the wall in a boys' rest room. Eric wasn't in trouble, like they were, but he wasn't any less miserable either.

The secretary emerged from the inner office. "Eric, Dr. Noble will see you now." While the two criminals breathed a sigh of relief at their temporary stay of execution, Eric rose and went into the office, where the dignified, gray-haired principal sat behind a desk.

"Hello, Eric," she said pleasantly. "Sit down." She

was smiling, but she was still pretty intimidating. "How can I help you?"

Eric sat, but he shifted around uncomfortably in his chair. "Um, it's about Adrian Peele. You asked me to be his big brother."

"Oh yes, of course. How are you getting along with our celebrity?"

"Not so great," Eric admitted. "He's—he's not exactly, well, I mean . . ." He struggled for the right words to describe Adrian, but he didn't want to seem uncooperative. "I just don't think it's going to work out, Dr. Noble."

Of course, that response wasn't enough to satisfy the demanding principal. "Can you tell me why?"

Eric tried. "He's not interested in having a big brother. He's not interested in *anything*! Like—like sports."

Dr. Noble smiled. "He's quite small, Eric. You can't expect him to go out for football or basketball."

"He could do gymnastics," Eric proposed. "I even invited him to come to my basketball practices just to watch. But he keeps saying no."

"Maybe he's just not into sports," Dr. Noble suggested.

"But like I said, Dr. Noble, he's not into anything. He doesn't want to play computer games, or go biking, or watch videos, and each time I suggest something, he looks at me like I'm boring him. He doesn't want a big brother, Dr. Noble. I don't think he wants any friends."

The principal pondered the problem. "This situation can't be easy for Adrian, Eric. Can you imagine what it must be like, being six years younger and two feet shorter than your classmates? He's probably afraid of being teased or pushed around. He could be shy."

"Shy," Eric repeated. That was the last word he'd use to describe Adrian.

Dr. Noble wasn't finished. "And remember, Adrian hasn't had much social interaction in his life. He was so much smarter than his peers, I'm sure he didn't have friends his own age. I would guess that he's been over-protected by his parents. And of course, he's been the focus of so much attention lately. He's probably suspicious of anyone who makes friendly overtures."

Eric slumped in his seat and shrugged in resignation. "What do you want me to do?"

"Just don't give up," Dr. Noble said. "Keep trying. Even if Adrian seems standoffish, it could be that he's simply not accustomed to having friends. Give him some time. I'm sure you'll be able to establish a relationship with him soon."

She rose from her chair. Eric knew this meant that their meeting was over. He got up too. "Okay," he said.

"Thank you, Dr. Noble." Mentally he added, Thanks for nothing. She'd been no help at all.

Leaving the office, he ran into a couple of pals, Kyle and Andy. "You in trouble?" Kyle asked, nodding toward the door Eric was coming from.

"Yeah," Eric muttered. "But not the usual kind. I was trying to get out of that big brother job, but Noble won't let me off the hook."

Andy was sympathetic. "So you still have to chase after that kid, huh? Man, I don't envy you. Did you hear what he said in homeroom this morning? The teacher asked him what would be his biggest challenge here at Parkside. He said it was a challenge trying to be tolerant of people with limited intelligence."

Eric wasn't surprised. He shook his head wearily. "Adrian sure knows how to win friends."

"I've got something even better on him," Kyle reported. "He's in my English class, and yesterday he announced that he'd already read all the assigned books. He told Ms. Weller he was surprised that ninth-graders were assigned juvenile books like *A Tale of Two Cities*."

"I'll bet Weller loved hearing that," Eric said.

"That's the weirdest part," Kyle said. "Here was this toad insulting her reading list, and she wasn't even angry! It's like she's so impressed with his brains, she doesn't care if he's rude and obnoxious."

"He's worse than obnoxious," Andy said. "I swear, he gives me the creeps, the way he looks at people. It's like he's some kind of demon."

Kyle snapped his fingers. "Hey, remember that old movie about the son of Satan? *The Omen?* Wasn't the kid named Adrian?"

"No, it was Damien," Eric said. But he could understand how Kyle could confuse the names—and the kids.

Parkside's own little demon was already seated when Eric entered his biology class. Other students were there too, perched at lab tables or just standing around shooting the breeze. No one was talking to Adrian.

The small boy sat alone at a table. He was bent over a spiral notebook, and he was scribbling something in it. Recalling Dr. Noble's words, Eric steeled himself, forced his lips into something that resembled a smile, and ambled over to the prodigy.

"Hi, Adrian."

No response. The only sign that Adrian might have heard Eric was the fact that he tried to cover what he was writing.

Eric sighed. "Adrian. I said hi."

The boy glanced up. Once again, Eric was struck by how totally ordinary the little genius looked. He was average size for his age, and his hair and eyes were the same shade of plain brown.

"What do you want?"

"Adrian, I don't *want* anything. I'm just saying hi."

Adrian looked at him, his face expressionless. That unblinking gaze was eerie. Eric ran his fingers through his hair and became aware that beads of sweat were forming on his forehead. This is ridiculous, he thought. He's an eight-year-old kid, for crying out loud! Why am I letting this infant make me so nervous? "Look, I just want to know how you're doing, that's all."

Adrian appeared to be considering the comment seriously, but his response wasn't what Eric expected. "You're contradicting yourself. You said, and I quote, 'Adrian, I don't *want* anything.' Then you said, 'I just want to know how you're doing.' Are you capable of hearing the discrepancy in your words?"

Eric could feel the blood rushing into his face. Fortunately for Adrian, their teacher came in at that moment.

Mrs. Pearlman looked tired. Their biology teacher was pregnant, and it seemed to Eric that she was visibly bigger each day. But she managed a bright smile when she looked at Adrian. "Good morning!"

Adrian didn't return the smile, but at least he nodded at the teacher. Eric slunk back to his own table. His lab partner, Alyssa, looked at him with sympathy. "Noble wouldn't let you drop the kid, huh?"

Eric didn't bother to answer—he knew that his expression said it all. He was feeling extremely frustrated. What did Dr. Noble expect from him, anyway? He wasn't a magician. He couldn't wave a wand and transform a snotty little brat into a normal human being. He'd been busting himself all week, trying to be a pal to Adrian, but he was sure now that it was a hopeless endeavor.

Mrs. Pearlman was talking, and Eric pushed thoughts of Adrian out of his head as he concentrated on taking notes. He had to admit, he was understanding a lot more since Jeremy had started tutoring him. Jeremy wasn't any more fun than Adrian was, but at least he could communicate information well. Eric was beginning to feel that he might actually get a handle on biology.

As usual, as soon as Mrs. Pearlman paused to take a breath, Jeremy's hand shot up. He never had a question for the teacher—he just liked commenting on whatever she was saying. He was always trying to impress her, and he usually succeeded.

"In regard to cell division," he began, "I happened to see a very interesting documentary on the Science Channel last night—" He didn't get any further. Several students started hissing and booing.

Jeremy frowned, and so did Mrs. Pearlman, but there

was a twinkle in her eye as she addressed the noisy classmates. "Isn't No-TV Week over yet?"

"Today's the last day," someone called out.

Jeremy spoke stiffly. "As I understand it, the purpose of No-TV Week is to encourage people to do something more productive with their time than sit in front of a television watching meaningless drivel. The documentary I refer to featured two Nobel Prize–winning physicists. It wasn't exactly *Dawson's Creek.*"

"Hey, you got something against *Dawson's Creek?*" an outraged girl demanded.

Jeremy looked pained. "I'm just using that as an example. My point is that there are some valuable programs on television."

Adrian spoke up. "There is nothing worth watching on television," he stated flatly.

Students looked at each other and rolled their eyes, but Mrs. Pearlman gazed at Adrian with interest. "What about news programs?"

"News on television has no value," Adrian said. "The medium trivializes the message. All information is compressed or expanded to fit into the format of the time allotted for the program. A newspaper provides more in-depth coverage. Of course, that is assuming that the TV viewer can also read."

It was the longest speech Eric had heard yet from Adrian. It was too weird—Adrian had the voice of a child, high-pitched and a little squeaky. But the words that came out of his mouth were barely understandable.

Eric did understand that last sentence, though—Adrian was implying that people who watched TV couldn't read. The mutterings around him were a clear indication that the others had caught Adrian's message too.

"Aw, come on, Adrian," a student remonstrated. "Are you telling me you never turn on your TV?"

"I don't have a television," Adrian replied. "In fact, there never has been one in my home."

Gasps of shock and disbelief filled the classroom. Mrs. Pearlman now looked even more intrigued. "Tell me, Adrian, did the lack of television encourage you to read more?" she asked. "Do you think it had any impact on your intellectual development?" Her hand was on her stomach as she spoke, and Eric had pity for the unborn child. Now the poor kid would probably never even get to watch *Sesame Street*.

Adrian responded to the question. "That would be difficult to assess. But the nature versus nurture argument is very interesting."

Mrs. Pearlman tore her eyes away from Adrian and addressed the rest of the class. "What Adrian refers to is an ongoing debate among scientists. It's not clear how much of who we are is based on our genetics and how much is based on our upbringing, our environment. We know, for example, that genetics are responsible for the color of our eyes. But what about musical talent? Are you born with a natural talent, or is it something you learn?"

She paused and looked thoughtful. "You know, this subject isn't a part of our regular curriculum, but it certainly ties into our discussions. I'm going to put some articles on reserve in the library, and I want everyone to read them by this time next week."

"In addition to the textbook?" someone asked in dismay.

"Yes."

This announcement was greeted with a chorus of groans. Mrs. Pearlman ignored them and turned back to Adrian with a big smile. "Thank you, Adrian. You're making a fine contribution to this class."

Eric could hear Alyssa making soft gagging noises. But it was Jeremy who was having the most interesting reaction. The tutor was staring at Mrs. Pearlman in dismay. It was clear that Adrian had usurped Jeremy's role as teacher's pet. And it was also clear that Jeremy wasn't happy about this.

Armed with her miniature tape recorder, a notepad, and a fine-line roller ball–style pen, Tasha surveyed the cafeteria. There was a particular table, way in the back and so far from the windows that, unless the cafeteria was unusually crowded, no one sat at it. And no one was sitting there now, except Adrian.

Tasha's heart ached for the poor kid. She'd heard Eric's stories, but she couldn't believe the little boy could be all that bad. Just because Adrian wasn't a jock, her narrow-minded brother couldn't communicate with him. Besides, Eric didn't have any patience with children.

Tasha hadn't yet managed to have a face-to-face meeting with Adrian. Since he was in the ninth grade, while she was in the seventh, they had no classes together. She'd caught glimpses of him only in the cafeteria, and he was always sitting with a teacher. This was the first time she'd seen him alone. It was just as well that she'd had to wait this long for an interview opportunity. Now that Adrian had had a week to settle down and get oriented, he'd probably be less intimidated and more open to her questions.

She moved closer to the table, but she didn't confront him immediately. As a journalist, she knew she had to learn as much as possible about her subject before interviewing him. So she hovered by the wall and simply observed him for a moment. Unobtrusively she made some notes on her pad.

Khaki pants, plaid shirt, high-top sneakers. Small, slim, narrow shoulders. Complexion pale—probably doesn't get outside much. Serious face. Reading a fat book.

She squinted, but she couldn't make out the title.

Eating a sandwich while he reads. (Note to me—find out what's in the sandwich.) Brought lunch from home. No lunchbox, plain brown-paper bag.

Most kids at Parkside bought the cafeteria lunch, even though it was usually terrible. But Adrian was still a child and probably fussy about his food. No eight-year-old would be content eating mystery meat. Or Parkside's most infamous dessert—brown stuff with white things in it. No one was ever sure if the white things were coconut, rice, or bugs.

Enough observation, she decided. With a bright smile, she strode over to his table. "Hi, Adrian!"

No response.

"Adrian?"

With obvious reluctance, he tore his eyes from the book and looked up. "Yes? What do you want?"

"I'm Tasha Morgan. Eric's sister."

Even as the words left her lips, she wished she hadn't uttered them. From what her brother had said, any connection to him wouldn't impress Adrian. Quickly she changed the subject. "Good book?" She could see the title now, and she read it out loud. "*Systematic Evaluation of Cell Division and Regeneration.* Wow. I guess that's not the latest Animorphs, huh?"

"What do you want?" he asked again.

She couldn't blame him for being hostile. She wondered if maybe his classmates had been giving him a hard time. Kids could be so insensitive if you were different.

"I was wondering if we could talk for a few minutes." She sat down across from him, even though he hadn't invited her to. He was just a little kid; he couldn't know anything about manners. "I'm a junior reporter for *The Parkside Journal.* That's not the school newspaper, you know. The school paper is called *The Parkside News,* and everyone calls it the *Snooze* because it's so boring. The *Journal* is a real community newspaper."

He didn't react to this information. Maybe she was overwhelming him, coming across like some sort of major school big shot or something. "I'd like to interview you for the *Journal,*" she told him.

"No, thank you," he said, and returned to his book.

"There's nothing to be afraid of; it won't be difficult," Tasha said quickly. "I'll just ask you some questions and you'll answer them. It'll be fun!" She showed him her tape recorder. "Look at this. It looks like a toy, doesn't it? I'll bet you've never seen such a tiny tape recorder before! But it really, truly works. I'll show you!" She hit Record and said, "Testing, one, two, three." Then she rewound the tape and pressed the Play button. Her own tinny voice could be heard, saying, "Testing, one, two, three."

"Now, you say something! Anything!" She hit Stop and then Record.

"Go away and leave me alone," he said.

She stopped the recorder, rewound, and hit Play. It wasn't until she heard his words again that she realized he hadn't been kidding.

She looked at him uncertainly. "I understand. We don't have to do this right now. Maybe you're just not in the mood to be interviewed today."

"That's right," Adrian said. "I'm not in the mood today. And I won't be in the mood tomorrow either. Or the day after that. Or ever."

The coldness in his voice startled her. "It won't take long," she began. "I just have—"

"It's already taken too long. For the past five minutes, I could have been reading my book. I am requesting that you go away and leave me alone. Or do I need to ask a cafeteria monitor to remove you forcibly?"

Tasha blinked. "A cafeteria monitor?" They were the kids who wore badges and were essentially responsible for breaking up food fights.

"You have three seconds to get away from me," Adrian said. "One . . ."

Tasha tried to control her temper. "Adrian, this is no way to act if you want to make friends in your new school."

"I'm not here to make friends," Adrian replied. "Two . . ."

"But, Adrian—"

"Three." He waved to a passing student who wore the insignia of the cafeteria patrol. "Monitor! Could you come here, please?"

Tasha snatched up her tape recorder. It took every ounce of her willpower to keep herself from using certain words and expressions that weren't exactly suitable for the ears of an eight-year-old. Meanwhile, the monitor had ambled over. Tasha recognized him as one of Eric's pals.

"What's the matter?" he asked Adrian. "This lady

trying to steal your lunch?" He chortled hysterically at his own remark.

"Oh, shut up," Tasha growled, and walked away.

Amy was waiting for her at their usual table. She took one look at Tasha's face and asked, "Who do you want to kill?"

"Adrian Peele," Tasha said through her teeth. As they got in line for their trays, she told Amy about the encounter she and Adrian had just had.

"You know," Tasha said as they returned to the table with the so-called food, "for once in my life, I actually agree with my brother. That kid is clueless."

"Really? Is he as awful as Eric says?" Amy asked.

"Worse. He's arrogant, he's egotistical, he's contemptuous . . ."

Amy grinned. "You're just looking for an excuse to show off your vocabulary again."

Tasha jabbed a fork into something green on her plate and actually ate it. "Amy, there's something very, very strange about that boy."

"Of course there is," Amy said agreeably. "He's a child prodigy. Tasha, an eight-year-old genius isn't going to act like an ordinary person."

"It's more than that," Tasha told her. "He's *creepy*. Remember when we watched that old horror movie

Village of the Damned? Remember those monster children with the glowing eyes?"

Amy nodded. "Are you telling me he has a golden glow in his pupils?"

"Not a glow, exactly. But I could swear I saw a glittery spark."

Amy burst out laughing. "Oh, come on, Tasha. He can't be that bad."

"Yeah, that's what I said too." Tasha speared another hunk of green stuff. "I guess I'll go back to writing about No-TV Week."

But the more she thought about that, the more unappealing and boring her original topic seemed.

A good reporter wouldn't give up so easily, Tasha thought. A good reporter would pursue her subject relentlessly until the subject broke down. The last person who interviewed Leonardo DiCaprio probably had to track him down to the ends of the earth. And Adrian Peele was no Leonardo DiCaprio.

Eric had told her that Adrian's last class was health education. That meant he'd be leaving school through the gymnasium exit. So at the end of the day, she rushed directly outside and positioned herself near the gym door, behind a pillar, where she could hide but still see everyone coming out. She assumed that a parent would be coming to pick Adrian up. Maybe if she asked the parent about doing an interview, Adrian could be talked into cooperating.

She didn't have to wait long. Adrian was one of the first students out the door. But he didn't remain in the area where kids waited to be picked up. He kept on walking.

Tasha looked around to see if she could spot Amy, but her friend hadn't emerged from the building yet. Tasha couldn't wait for her. Adrian was moving quickly around the side of the school.

Keeping enough distance so he wouldn't be aware she was following his footsteps, she started after him. She couldn't imagine where he was going. Did he live so close to the school that he could walk home by himself?

But Adrian wasn't going home. Behind Parkside, he walked around the football field and made his way toward a building that Tasha knew well. She should have guessed this was where he'd be heading. Where else would a child prodigy go after school? The public library, of course.

The library's parking lot faced the middle-school building. Tasha kept her distance, dodging between cars to stay hidden. To her surprise, Adrian didn't start around the library to get to its front door. Instead, he made his way directly to the fire escape on the side of the building.

She crouched behind a station wagon and watched him as he climbed the fire escape. What was he planning to do, break into the library? Why couldn't he just walk through the door like a normal person?

Because he wasn't a normal person. She had to keep reminding herself of that. And watching him now, she was even more sure of it.

Adrian climbed all the way to the top of the fire escape. Then he sat down on the landing and stayed there. Tasha watched for a while, but nothing happened. He just continued to sit and stare off into space.

After ten minutes of observation, Tasha didn't know what to think. Adrian hadn't moved. She wished she had Amy's talent for seeing over long distances—at least then she could read his expression. Or even see what he was looking at.

But maybe he wasn't looking at anything. So what was he doing up there? Contacting a UFO to come take him back to whatever planet he came from? She smiled at her thought and then, just as quickly, stopped smiling. The kid was very, very weird. So weird that she wouldn't be at all surprised to learn that he had some sort of connection to an alien entity.

She continued to wait, her heart pounding. Every

now and then she glanced upward, not sure what she might see. No UFOs appeared. But that didn't mean Adrian wasn't involved in some sort of nonhuman communication.

He remained on the fire escape for an hour. Then he climbed back down. Now he seemed to be going around to the front door of the library. Tasha followed, edging around the side of the building.

But Adrian didn't go into the library. He stood in front of the main door for about a minute. Then a big car pulled up. Tasha could just make out the figure of a large woman behind the wheel. She didn't look at all like an alien.

Adrian went to the passenger side of the car, opened the door, and got in. And the car pulled away.

three

Amy didn't find Tasha's story all that intriguing.

"Maybe he was just thinking," she suggested. "Very intelligent people do that once in a while, you know."

Tasha made a face at her. "But why go to a fire escape to think? It can't be very comfortable sitting on metal."

The two girls were sprawled across the twin beds in Amy's room. Amy stared up at the ceiling and tried to come up with a reason for Adrian—or anyone—to hang out on the library fire escape. "He needs a place to be alone," she guessed. "And he doesn't want to go home because, because . . . I know! Because his mother worries about him and hovers over him. She watches him every minute and keeps asking if he's okay." Amy knew all about mothers who worried and hovered.

As if on cue, the voice of the mother she knew best floated up the stairs. "Girls! Are you hungry? Do you want a snack?" Tasha leaped eagerly off the bed.

"Don't get excited," Amy advised her. "It's just granola and fruit. My mom's on a health-food kick."

Tasha's nose wrinkled. "Why? It's not like you can get any healthier than you already are."

Amy had no answer for that. What Tasha had just said was undeniably true. And Nancy knew it better than anyone else.

The woman Amy called Mom had been one of the original scientists connected to Project Crescent. The scientists had been told that their cloning experiments were expected to produce new information about genetic disorders so that future generations wouldn't suffer.

But the scientists discovered that this was not the goal of the project at all. A secret government organization was attempting to create perfect life-forms—with the ultimate goal of generating a master race. And the scientists knew that the existence of a master race could present frightening, horrifying possibilities.

They all agreed that the project had to be terminated. But they couldn't destroy the infant lives, the twelve Amys, who were the result of their experiments. So they removed the infants from the laboratory and then set off an explosive device that demolished the building. They hoped the organization would assume that the infants had died in the explosion.

Meanwhile, the tiny clones had been sent to various adoption agencies all over the world. That is, all but one were sent away. Nancy Candler had bonded with one clone in particular—Amy, Number Seven. She'd taken her home to raise as her own daughter.

In a way, Nancy had less to worry about than the mother of an ordinary kid. Amy's genetic makeup made it virtually impossible for her to get sick. Even if she was injured, she recovered much faster and more easily than any regular person. She was stronger, faster, and capable of reacting and responding more quickly than anyone.

But in another way, she was more vulnerable than other children. The organization never believed that the clones had perished in the explosion, and they were still out there, looking for Amys. So Nancy Candler did have cause to worry, and Amy couldn't really blame her for occasionally hovering.

Maybe the mothers of all special children were like

that. If so, Amy could understand why Adrian might feel the need once in a while to hide on a fire escape.

"How was school today?" Nancy asked the girls as she placed a big bowl of crunchy brown stuff on the table.

"Okay," Amy replied. "Tasha met the prodigy."

"What's he like?"

"Weird," Tasha said. "And rude. He won't talk to anyone. He sits by himself in the cafeteria and writes in a little notebook."

"He sounds like Harriet the Spy," Nancy commented. She set a bowl of oranges down next to the granola and left the dining room.

Amy considered that. *Harriet the Spy* had been her favorite book when she was younger, and she enjoyed rereading it once in a while. She could still get into the story of the girl who spied on people, writing about them in her secret notebook, and then was publicly humiliated when her notebook was discovered.

"You know," she told Tasha, "anyone who loves *Harriet the Spy* couldn't be all bad."

"Just because he acts like her doesn't mean he loves the book," Tasha pointed out. She tried the granola. "Yuck."

Nancy returned to the room with a stack of books

in her arms. She glanced at the untouched granola. "There's milk in the refrigerator, if you want to add some," she said.

Personally, Amy didn't think milk would do much to improve the granola. "Where are you going?" she asked her mother.

"To the library. These books are way overdue."

Amy and Tasha looked at each other, and Amy knew they were both thinking the same thing. "Can we come along?" Amy asked.

Nancy was surprised. "You were just at the library two days ago. Have you finished those books already?"

"Sure," Amy lied. "I'm a fast reader. You know that."

"Yes, I know you're *capable* of fast reading," Nancy replied dryly. "I just haven't seen you take advantage of that particular talent lately. You two can tag along, however. But I'm not staying there. I'm just dropping the books off."

"That's okay," Amy told her. "We'll walk home."

When they entered the public library a while later, the girls went to the paperback rack in the young adult section. There they waited for a few minutes, until they felt sure Nancy had completed her business, paid her fines, and left. Then they went out of the building and walked around to the back.

Tasha pointed at the fire escape. "He was on the third-floor landing," she told Amy.

Amy gazed up. "I wonder if he could see something from there."

"I don't know," Tasha replied.

"You didn't climb up to see?" Amy teased. Tasha had a notorious fear of heights. Even after a week at Wilderness Adventure had forced her to overcome her anxieties, her newfound courage hadn't lasted very long.

Fortunately, Amy had no problem with heights. She scrambled up the metal rungs until she reached the third-floor platform. "What direction was he looking in?" she called down to Tasha.

Tasha pointed, and Amy turned in that direction. She could see only some rooftops, nothing interesting. Then it occurred to her that Adrian was a lot shorter than she was. She crouched down. Now there was an apartment building window in her line of sight. The building was close, and the curtains were open, so even without using her super-vision, Amy could see into a room. And directly into the screen of a television.

The TV was on. Amy watched for a moment as a cartoon mouse with a frying pan chased a cat. The mouse caught up to the cat and banged him with the pan, flattening his head like a pancake. In typical cartoon style, the head then bounced back to normal size.

Focusing and using her extraordinary vision, Amy was able to make out the channel number. She knew that this channel showed cartoons twenty-four hours a day. It had been in the news lately because some parents objected to the violence of the cartoons it presented.

She couldn't see if anyone was in the room watching the TV. It was possible that no one was there. She recalled that the report she'd read mentioned how some kids with their own sets left the TV permanently on and tuned to this channel.

She watched for a few more minutes. The cat responded to the head-banging by feeding the mouse poisoned cheese. Then the mouse set fire to the cat's pillow. The cat retaliated by setting a bomb in the mouse's hole.

Amy didn't wait to see the mouse blown to bits. She climbed back down the fire escape.

Tasha was waiting expectantly. "Well?"

"I think he was looking into a window," Amy told her.

Tasha's eyes gleamed. "Really? He was spying! Or maybe someone was passing him messages."

"Right," Amy said. "Instructions on how to blow up a mouse."

"Huh?"

"He was watching Channel Six. At least, that's what it looked like to me."

Tasha was confused. "Why would he climb up a fire escape to watch cartoons on someone's TV set?"

Amy recalled what Eric had told her just that afternoon. "He doesn't have a TV at home. He told his class that there was nothing worth watching. You know, I think that's kind of cute. He pretends to be too intellectual to watch TV, and then he sneaks up the fire escape to veg out on cartoons."

Tasha disagreed. "I don't think that's so cute. I did a lot of reading about Channel Six when I was getting ready to write the No-TV Week article. A lot of people think TV shows like that influence kids. Maybe watching all that violence is what makes him so nasty."

"Well, at least now you know he isn't getting any interplanetary messages," Amy said. "Under all that intelligence, he just might be a normal little kid."

"A normal kid with an abnormal attitude," Tasha grumbled.

"Maybe he's just lonely," Amy suggested. "He's been

treated so differently all his life, he doesn't know how to make friends."

"That's the understatement of the century," Tasha said.

Amy thought about this. "I think we should help him out," she said.

"How?" Tasha asked suspiciously.

"Tomorrow's Saturday. Let's do something with Adrian."

Tasha stared at her in dismay. "You want to waste a Saturday on that little creep?"

"We can arrange an outing," Amy said. "You, me, Eric, and Adrian. We can go to the zoo. Or maybe we can play miniature golf."

"And just why do we want to do that?"

"Because we're nice people."

"We're not *that* nice."

Amy came up with another reason. "Because I feel sorry for him," she admitted. "And a little guilty. I should have tried harder to meet him by now. He needs to know another person who's different."

Tasha was shocked. "You're not going to tell him about yourself, are you?"

"Of course not. But maybe he'll feel that I'm just naturally more sympathetic. And anyway, Dr. Noble wants Eric to work harder at being a big brother to Adrian. So he needs to get more involved with him."

"Okay, you've got a reason to play with Adrian, and so does Eric," Tasha said. "But I don't."

"You want to get an interview, don't you? You'll have a much better chance if you hang out with him."

Tasha considered this. "But even if we offer to take him somewhere, there's no guarantee he'll agree to it. We can't force him to spend time with us."

"But it won't be his decision to make," Amy replied with a grin. "I'll bet his parents want him to have friends."

It wasn't all that difficult to organize. Amy got her mother to call Adrian's mother and propose the outing. And on Saturday afternoon, with the address of the Peele home in hand, Amy took off with Tasha and Eric.

Eric was not in a good mood. "I can't believe I'm giving up a Saturday for that brat. What a waste."

"It will be a waste if you go with that attitude," Amy reprimanded him. "Look, I know it's not going to be easy to connect with Adrian, but we have to try."

"You have no idea how not easy it's going to be," Tasha warned her.

It wasn't a long walk to Adrian's home, but none of them had been on this particular street before. "Nice neighborhood," Eric commented as they walked down the block, consulting the numbers on the houses. "Almost looks like Beverly Hills."

Amy agreed. The houses weren't mansions, but they were pretty grand. Even though the street was in the Parkside school district, she didn't know anyone who lived here. She figured any kids from this area would probably go to private schools.

The Peele house was particularly nice. "They must be rich," Tasha said.

But the woman who answered the door didn't look rich—mainly because she wore a frilly white apron with the name of a local coffee shop embroidered on it.

"Mrs. Peele?" Amy asked uncertainly.

"Yes, I'm Adrian's mother," the woman said. "Come in. Thank you for being so prompt. I wanted to meet you all before I left for work." She ushered them into the living room. "Adrian? Your friends are here."

Adrian didn't seem particularly eager to see his so-called friends. He glared at them balefully and didn't even say hello.

"What do you young people have planned for today?" Mrs. Peele asked.

"We thought we'd take Adrian to the zoo," Eric told her. "We'd have him back here by five o'clock."

"Oh, no, that's much too late," Mrs. Peele said. "Adrian has a clinic appointment at three-thirty."

"Clinic?" Amy asked politely.

"Yes! The Clinic for the Study of Highly Gifted Children." Mrs. Peele spoke with pride, as if she assumed they knew about the place. Amy had never heard of it.

"Where's this clinic?" she asked.

"On Cloverdale Road. We're very lucky to have such a prestigious institute so close by. And we're thrilled that Adrian was accepted as a candidate! It opened only a month ago, and it's already considered very elite."

"That's nice," Amy said. She looked at Adrian. "Do you like going to this clinic?"

Adrian just looked bored.

Eric glanced at his watch. "Well, if he has an appointment at three-thirty, that gives us only two hours. It takes half an hour just to get to the zoo."

"I have an idea," Mrs. Peele said. "There's a very nice playground not far from here."

Eric nodded. "Yeah, I know the place. We can rent in-line skates."

"Isn't that dangerous?" Mrs. Peele asked anxiously.

"Not if you wear pads and a helmet," Eric assured her. "And we can rent all that stuff there."

A man with a pleasant face came into the room, and

Mrs. Peele introduced him as Adrian's father. "Martin, these are Adrian's new friends from Parkside Middle School. They're taking him to the playground."

"That's nice," Mr. Peele said, shaking hands with each of them.

"You have a lovely home," Tasha said.

"Thank you," he said. "We moved here a month ago."

"Oh, you're new to Los Angeles?" Amy asked.

"No, we lived on the other side of the city. In Vista View Heights."

It was decided that the kids would walk to the playground and Mr. Peele would pick Adrian up there to take him to his clinic appointment. Mrs. Peele walked them to the door. "You will watch out for him, won't you?" she asked anxiously.

"Of course," Amy assured her. "And don't worry! We'll have fun."

They hadn't even reached the playground before she began to doubt her own words. Adrian's expression remained grim, and he clearly wasn't up for any conversation.

"Does your mother work at the Happy Diner?" Amy asked him.

"Yes."

"They have the best blueberry muffins," she said enthusiastically. "Do you eat a lot of those?"

"No."

"What does your father do?" she asked. "Does he work?"

"Yes."

"Where?"

"Bank."

At least that explained the fancy house.

"What do you want to do when you grow up?" Tasha asked sweetly.

He gave her a withering look and didn't bother to answer.

It became clear that Adrian's parents had insisted on his coming out with them. He had absolutely no interest in being at the playground. Once there, he planted himself on a bench and refused to budge.

Eric and Tasha went off to rent equipment, and Amy stayed with Adrian. She tried to get some sort of communication going.

"This clinic you go to," she said. "What do you do there? Take tests?"

He didn't respond. He pulled a paperback book out of his jacket pocket and opened it. Amy saw the title. *"The Double Helix,"* she read aloud. "Doesn't that have something to do with the discovery of DNA?"

She could have sworn that he actually looked at her. "You know about DNA? That's not in the seventh-grade curriculum."

"Well, no, but I think it's interesting."

Eric and Tasha returned on in-line skates. "You sure you don't want to skate, Adrian?" Eric asked.

"I want to read," Adrian replied. He rubbed his eyes and frowned. "But there's a terrible glare here."

"Well, I can't move the sun for you," Eric said.

"But we could move the bench into the shade," Amy told him. "Come on, Eric, help me lift it." She could have lifted the bench on her own, but she knew better than to show off her unusual strength in public.

At least Adrian had the courtesy to get off the bench so she and Eric could move it. The bench turned out to be made of metal, and it was pretty heavy. Eric grunted several times as he lifted his end. Adrian watched Amy, and now she really saw a glimmer of interest in his eyes.

"You're very strong for your size," he said.

"Yes, I am," Amy acknowledged. Adrian continued to stare at her, so she had to say something else. "My mother's strong too. I guess it runs in the family."

"So it's genetic," Adrian said.

"Yeah, I guess so." She and Eric and placed the bench in the shade, and Adrian sat down.

"I want a Popsicle," Adrian declared.

"Okay," Amy said. "There's an ice cream stand over there. Let's go."

"I want to read," Adrian said. "You go and get me a Popsicle. My first choice is passion fruit. If they don't have passion fruit, get me lime."

"You could say please," Tasha remarked. But Adrian was already engrossed in his book and ignored her words.

Amy tried to excuse his lack of manners. "He's just a little kid," she whispered to Tasha. "Watch him while I get the Popsicle." Meanwhile, Eric took off on his skates as Amy walked around the playground to the ice cream stand. There was no passion fruit or lime, so she bought raspberry.

When she returned, Tasha was trying desperately to get Adrian into some kind of conversation. "Do you meet lots of other smart kids at your clinic?" she was asking.

He said nothing and accepted the Popsicle from Amy. Then he actually spoke—but not to say thank you. "I don't like raspberry," he said, and tossed the Popsicle onto the ground. Amy had to work at restraining her temper. Tasha looked like she was about to explode, so Amy grabbed her arm and pulled her away a step.

"Be cool," Amy warned.

But Tasha was beyond cool. "You see what I mean? Do you believe me now? He's horrible!"

"There has to be a reason," Amy murmured. "Even little kids aren't *that* rude."

"What are we going to do with him for two hours?" Tasha wanted to know.

Amy looked for Eric. He'd found some guys he knew, and they were happily attempting to perform tricks on their skates. It was obvious that *he* wasn't going to help them out.

She and Tasha spent another ten minutes trying to engage Adrian in dialogue. Finally they gave up and let him read in silence. But Amy had to stay close, to keep an eye on him. And Tasha, being her best friend, stayed with her. They sat on the grass a few yards from the bench and aimlessly peeled dandelion stems.

Finally Adrian's father arrived. The girls got up. "Hello, Mr. Peele," Amy said. "Adrian didn't feel like skating."

Mr. Peele didn't seem surprised. "Our boy has a mind of his own, that's for sure. Ready to go, Adrian?"

"I want to finish this chapter," Adrian said.

While they waited, Amy attempted to talk with Mr. Peele. "Adrian says you work in a bank. That must be exciting. Lots of big money deals and all."

"I do work in a bank," Mr. Peele said. "I'm a teller at Southside Federal."

Amy tried not to let her surprise show. She didn't know much about banking, but she knew that being a teller wasn't quite the same as being a bank president.

On the way home, she remarked on this to Tasha and Eric. "If his father's a bank teller and his mother is a waitress, how can they afford that fancy house?"

"Maybe they inherited it," Eric suggested. "And that's why they moved from Vista View Heights."

"What do you know about Vista View Heights?" Tasha asked.

"My Scout troop did some volunteer landscaping work there once," Eric told her. "It's a subdivision for people who don't make very much money." His mood had improved considerably. "You know, that wasn't so bad today."

"Not bad for *you*," Tasha countered. "You didn't spend any time with Adrian at all!"

Eric wasn't offended by her criticism. "That's okay," he said cheerfully. "At least I can tell Dr. Noble I took him to the playground."

"Great," Tasha grumbled to Amy. "We do all the work and he gets all the credit."

Amy couldn't argue with that. It hadn't been an easy day for her and Tasha. But still, she had to admit, there was something about Adrian that was sort of interesting.

Or at least, sort of odd.

four

To Eric's eyes, Mrs. Pearlman looked twice as big on Monday as she had on Friday. When she came into their biology class, she had one hand under her stomach, as if she needed the extra support just to hold it up. There were dark circles under her eyes, and she looked tired. Still, she managed a wan smile when someone asked, "Mrs. Pearlman, are you going to have triplets?"

"No. According to my doctor, this is just one very big baby."

"Do you know if you're having a boy or a girl?" Eric's lab partner, Alyssa, asked.

Eric couldn't resist answering. "Oh, sure, it's probably going to be one or the other."

Mrs. Pearlman's lips twitched, but she ignored Eric and answered Alyssa. "It's a boy. I had an amniocentesis test. Do you know what that is?" Some students didn't, so she explained. "Some fluid was taken from my womb, and it was analyzed to see if the baby could have certain medical problems. An added benefit of the test is that it also tells you the sex of the child."

"Your baby doesn't have any medical problems, does he?" Alyssa asked.

"No, thank goodness. But it's important to have information like that as early as possible. It's amazing what medical science can do now for the unborn child. Did you know that some medical conditions can be cured or corrected even before birth, while the baby is still in the womb?"

Jeremy's hand shot up. "But the new medical technology has drawbacks, too," he said. "Serious ethical questions have been raised."

"Can you give us an example, Jeremy?" Mrs. Pearlman asked.

He nodded importantly. "In some countries, where female children aren't valued as highly as male children, people could learn the sex of the fetus and take advantage of this information to prevent the birth of a female child. And there are other, more frightening possibilities."

Eric leaned back in his chair and stifled a yawn. He knew from experience that Jeremy was about to go into one of his long lectures and wouldn't stop until Mrs. Pearlman cut him off.

But Mrs. Pearlman didn't have to do that this time. Adrian broke into the lecture.

"Actually, the potential benefits of the new medical technology far outweigh the drawbacks. We will not only be able to predict a child's condition, we may be able to directly influence the condition."

"*We?*" a student asked sarcastically. "Are you going to be involved in this, Adrian?"

Adrian looked at him coldly. "I am referring to the scientific community, of course. Research is currently being conducted in the manipulation of genes and ways the genetic makeup of a human can be controlled."

"You're very interested in genetics, aren't you?" Mrs. Pearlman asked.

"Yes," Adrian replied. "I am currently a subject in a clinical study regarding the nature and the causes of unusually high intelligence. It is hoped that once we understand why I am a genius, other children might have the potential to be like me."

A titter went through the class. Mrs. Pearlman frowned. "Class, Adrian isn't bragging. He's stating a fact. Intelligence tests have confirmed that he is indeed in the genius category. And it would be very interesting to a new parent like me to know whether he inherited his genes from his parents or whether his intelligence was nurtured in the home environment."

Eric found himself actually listening to this discussion with interest. He had met Adrian's parents, and they didn't seem like geniuses. And Adrian had grown up in Vista View Heights. As far as Eric knew, that was a very ordinary suburban area.

"What sorts of tests are being conducted in your study, Adrian?" Mrs. Pearlman asked.

It was as if a shade had been drawn across Adrian's face. His expression went blank, and all he said was, "It would be too complicated to explain here."

Alyssa leaned to whisper in Eric's ear. "That kid is unreal! It's like he's come right out and said we're too dumb to understand!"

What was even more unreal, Eric thought, was the fact that he was implying that Mrs. Pearlman, a biology teacher, wouldn't understand. But Mrs. Pearlman wasn't offended. She just instructed the class to open their textbooks and began talking about the day's reading assignment.

Alyssa whispered to Eric again. "You're his big brother. You should tell him to get his act together."

Eric didn't think Adrian would appreciate—or *take*—any advice coming from him. But on the other hand, this was the kind of help Dr. Noble wanted him to give, so that Adrian could adjust to his new environment.

The principal had called Eric into her office that very morning, during homeroom. She'd heard from Mrs. Peele that Eric had taken Adrian to the playground on Saturday, and she was pleased. She encouraged Eric to do more activities with Adrian. And although the idea didn't appeal to Eric at all, he knew saying so wasn't a good way to score points with the principal—especially when he had all those demerits for tardiness on his permanent record. So when class ended, he headed over to Adrian's desk, where the boy was putting his textbook and his notebook away in his briefcase.

But someone else got there first.

"I'm intrigued by this clinical study you're in," Jeremy was saying to Adrian. "I can understand your reluctance to speak about it in front of the others. It's unlikely that they could understand it. But I want to know more. In fact, I may be interested in volunteering myself as a subject."

"You won't be able to participate in the study," Adrian said.

"Why not? Aren't they looking for more subjects?"

"Yes, they're always looking for subjects. But you don't meet the qualifications."

"Because of my age?" Jeremy asked.

"No," Adrian replied. "You're just not smart enough."

There was no mistaking the shock that appeared on Jeremy's face. Or the fury that followed. Eric didn't think Jeremy could get violent, but he stepped in quickly anyway.

"Adrian, Jeremy's very smart," he told him. "In fact, he's my tutor in this class."

Adrian wasn't impressed. "Then you're even less intelligent than I thought you were," he said, looking directly at Eric. With that, he hoisted his briefcase and left the room. But now Eric was feeling pretty furious himself, and he ran after the boy.

When he caught up to him, he spoke the way his own father had spoken to him when he was a little kid. "Adrian, that was not nice behavior."

Adrian ignored him and kept on walking.

"Adrian! Are you listening to me?"

Adrian stopped and turned toward him. "Are you going to say anything worth listening to?"

Eric clenched his fists and held them back. He thought about Dr. Noble's suggestion that morning.

He thought about the demerits on his permanent record. Through teeth clenched as tight as his fists, he said, "The Parkside talent show is tonight. Want me to take you?"

He expected Adrian to turn him down flatly and rudely. But the kid actually looked thoughtful.

"A talent show," he said. "That could be interesting. Yes, you may take me there."

As if he was doing Eric a big favor!

Nancy Candler poked her head into Amy's room. "Are you ready?"

"Five minutes," Amy promised.

"What's going on at school tonight?" Nancy asked.

"It's the annual talent show," Amy told her.

Mild alarm crossed Nancy's face. "You're not a part of it, are you?"

"No," Amy assured her. "I'm just in the audience with everyone else."

"I'll be waiting in the car," Nancy told her, and left.

Wistfully Amy thought how cool it would be to get up in front of everyone and do something spectacular. Like perform a circus acrobatic trick, swinging on a bar high above the auditorium, throwing herself into the air, executing a quadruple flip that took her across the room and then catching another bar. She'd never done that before, but knowing her strength and perfect timing, she knew she could. It would undoubtedly impress her classmates. But it would also raise a lot of questions that she wouldn't be able to answer.

She could hear her mother honking the car horn outside. Quickly she tied the drawstring of her skirt and ran down the stairs. Outside, Tasha and Eric were coming out of their front door, and they joined Amy and her mother in the car.

"How was your session with Jeremy?" Amy asked Eric.

"Not great. He was in a bad mood. In biology today, Adrian told him he wasn't smart enough to come to his clinic and be tested for genius status."

"What clinic is that?" Nancy asked.

"It's called the Clinic for the Study of Highly Gifted Children," Amy told her.

"I've never heard of it," Nancy remarked.

"Really? Mrs. Peele said it's a big deal, very elite."

"That's possible," her mother acknowledged. "I'm not very familiar with that kind of institution."

"Hey, I'll bet *you* could get into that study," Eric told Amy.

"I'm not so sure about that," Nancy said.

"Mom! Why not?"

Her mother glanced away from the road to give

her a teasing smile. "You have the potential to be a genius, sweetie. But you don't always live up to your potential!"

"I wonder if I could be accepted," Tasha said thoughtfully.

"Get real," Eric scoffed. "You're no genius."

"I'm unusually talented in some areas," Tasha reminded him. "My teachers say I have an extraordinary vocabulary."

"Gee, you could be performing tonight," Eric said. "Get up on the stage and recite words no one understands. Wow, I bet you'd get a standing ovation."

"Okay, children, that's enough teasing," Amy declared. "Mom, it's the third house on the right."

Nancy pulled into the driveway of the Peele home. Mrs. Peele must have been watching from the window, because the door opened immediately. She escorted Adrian, who was clutching his briefcase, to the car and tried to kiss him on the forehead. Adrian squirmed away.

"Could Adrian sit in the front seat?" she asked Nancy. "He has a tendency to get carsick."

Amy hopped out of the front and squeezed into the back with Tasha and Eric. She grinned at Tasha and knew that Tasha was thinking the same thing she was. Getting carsick was such a little-kid thing to do. It fit right in with the cartoon watching. Again, Amy realized Adrian was just a child after all.

Nancy dropped them off at the gym entrance. Amy always thought it felt so different coming to school at night. Outside lights framed the doors and cast purple shadows on the brick walls. The kids going into the building were dressed better than they were usually dressed for classes.

Inside, the gymnasium had been converted to an auditorium. The floor was covered with neat rows of folding chairs. Colored Christmas lights framed the stage.

"Isn't this nice?" Amy asked.

Adrian looked at her as if she'd just asked a very stupid question.

"Do you know anyone who's performing tonight?" Eric asked Amy.

"Jake Oldham from my homeroom is doing some sort of magic act," Amy replied. "And there's Jeanine, of course."

"Of course," Tasha echoed. "Miss Look-at-Me-at-All-Times. What's she going to do?"

"I don't know," Amy said. "She wanted to figure skate, but Dr. Noble wouldn't let her make ice on the stage."

As they worked their way down the aisle in search of

seats, Adrian's lack of popularity was apparent. Amy caught a few whispered comments, and there were a couple of remarks that even a person without super-hearing could catch.

"He's supposed to be a genius," one girl said to another. "But he has a retarded personality."

Amy looked at Adrian anxiously. He had to have heard that. But he didn't seem to care. Clearly, popularity meant nothing to him.

They found four seats together in the middle of the auditorium. Adrian went into the row first, followed by Eric, Amy, and Tasha. Amy picked up the program from her seat, but there was no time to look at it. The school band struck up familiar chords.

Amy, Tasha, and Eric rose. "Get up, Adrian, it's the school song," Eric said.

Adrian didn't budge. He remained in his seat, opened his briefcase, and took out a book. Amy silently read the title: *Investigations of Complex Molecular Structure*. Didn't Adrian ever read anything normal, like a comic book?

They finished singing "Parkside, O Parkside, My Heart Is True to Thee" and sat down. Dr. Noble came out onto the stage.

"Good evening, students, and welcome to the annual Parkside Middle School Talent Show. I'm sure you'll be as excited and impressed as I am with the quality of talent we have here. And if there are any Hollywood talent scouts in the audience, I have bad news for you. I'm afraid our performers are too busy with schoolwork to become big stars now."

The audience laughed politely at the principal's little joke. Dr. Noble then introduced the master of ceremonies, a ninth-grade boy, who then introduced the first act.

Amy leaned across Eric. "Adrian, put that book away. You're being very rude."

To her surprise, Adrian closed his book. She wasn't sure if that was because he was following her command, or simply because the first performers had taken the stage.

The performers were two eighth-grade girls, who proceeded to lip-synch their way through a song by Brandy and Monica that had been popular the year before. All the girls did was move their lips, which didn't require much talent. Amy couldn't really blame Adrian for returning to his book.

He closed the book again when the second act was introduced. This was Amy's classmate Jake with his magic show. Amy thought he was pretty good. But obviously Adrian wasn't intrigued. He went back to reading right away.

Nothing seemed to appeal to Adrian. He read through the performance of five boys in a breakdance routine, a tap-dancing girl, and six kids performing a scene from *Grease*. He did glance up when a ninth-grade girl performed a ballet solo, but when she wobbled on her toes he lost interest. He completely ignored the seventh-grade comedian.

What would it take to impress him? Amy wondered. She found out eventually. Toward the end of the show, a boy came out onto the stage with a violin. As he played, he was honored with Adrian's complete attention.

As the audience applauded the boy's performance, Amy leaned over toward Adrian. "He's good, huh?"

Adrian actually answered her. "He has a natural talent. That's interesting."

"Do you play an instrument?" Amy asked him.

Adrian didn't respond. He was looking at the program, and he made a check mark next to the violinist's name. Maybe he thought the violinist might be intelligent enough to be worthy of his friendship, Amy speculated.

He didn't show much interest in Jeanine's act. Since she hadn't been allowed to figure skate, Jeanine had decided to show off her gymnastic skills. She did a floor exercise with some nice twists.

Once more Amy tried to connect with Adrian. "Jeanine and I used to take gymnastics together," she told him. "I don't really like her very much, but she's doing a good routine so far."

She spoke too soon. The words had barely left her lips when Jeanine tripped over her own feet. The audience was polite enough not to laugh, but Amy could see Jeanine's face go red.

Amy almost felt sympathy for her. "She must have been nervous," she murmured to Tasha.

"Maybe," Tasha replied. "Or maybe there's another reason why she fell."

"Like what?"

Tasha spoke ominously. "Remember Melissa Mitchell?"

That wasn't a name Amy was likely to forget. Melissa had been a student at Parkside. After a car accident, she'd had some sort of brain operation that resulted in a weird side effect. She developed telekinesis, the ability to move things—and people—with her mind, just by looking at them and concentrating. Amy, Eric, and Tasha had been forced to risk their own lives to save the student body from Melissa's awesome power.

"What does Jeanine's fall have to do with Melissa Mitchell?"

Tasha lowered her voice. "Adrian was looking at her when she fell."

"Tasha," Amy said sternly, "save your imagination for creative writing, okay?" She just didn't think it was all that likely they'd run into two telekinetic people in one year.

Of course, she agreed with Tasha that Adrian wasn't exactly normal. But then, neither was Amy, and that was why she was determined to make every effort to be Adrian's friend. There could be so many reasons why he'd developed such an unpleasant personality. She'd give him another chance. And another, and another.

She had an opportunity the very next day. In the school cafeteria at lunchtime, she saw Adrian sitting at his usual place. And as usual, he was writing in his notebook. She watched as two boys approached him. One looked over his shoulder, trying to read what Adrian was writing. The other grabbed a cookie from Adrian's brown bag.

Amy moved quickly—or as quickly as she could allow herself to move, taking into account the fact that there were a lot of people around. She confronted the two boys.

"Knock it off," she said sharply. "Put the cookie back."

One of the boys laughed. "Who are you, the cafeteria queen? You're not even a monitor!"

"That's true," Amy said, "but I can make a citizen's arrest and drag you to Dr. Noble's office."

The boy continued to laugh. "I'd like to see you try." He grabbed Adrian's notebook out of his hands. Adrian let out a squeal.

You just made my day, Amy thought. She grabbed the boy's wrist. No one could see how tightly she was squeezing, but the boy could certainly feel the pressure. He let out a squeal even louder than Adrian's and dropped the notebook on the floor.

"Thank you," Amy said sweetly. She picked up the notebook and gave it back to Adrian. The two boys beat a hasty retreat.

She was pleased to see some real regard in Adrian's eyes. "That was a cry of pain," he said. "You must have hurt him."

"I might have squeezed his wrist a little too hard," Amy replied carelessly.

"But you're half his size! You're really unusually strong."

Amy brushed off his observation. "Can I sit down with you?" He nodded, so she did.

Then she began her prepared speech. "You know, Adrian, I can understand that it's difficult for you to be here at Parkside. And you think the only way you can deal with it is by being rude and nasty to everyone. But that's not necessary. There are jerks here, sure, but there are nice people too. Me, and Eric, and Tasha . . . we all want to be your friend. Give us a chance, okay?"

He gazed at her steadily. She tried to ignore the creepy feeling he gave her, like he was scrutinizing her.

"I'm not interested in Eric or Tasha," he said finally. "But you and I, perhaps we can be friends."

Amy was delighted. At least this was a start. "Great. Would you like to do something after school?"

"Today?" he asked. "I can't."

She remembered what she'd seen on the fire escape. "Are you going to the library?"

"No, I have an appointment at the clinic."

"Oh." Amy looked at him with concern. "Adrian, this clinic you go to . . . what happens there? Does a doctor examine you? Do you take tests?"

Adrian didn't reply. He opened his notebook and gave it his full attention.

Amy had a flashback—herself, under the supervision of a doctor. Being poked and prodded, examined and tested . . . the memory made her shudder.

"Adrian," she said urgently, "is something being done to you that you don't want? You can tell me."

But not that particular day. He was looking past her,

and Amy turned to see Tasha standing there. "Hi," Tasha said. "What's up?"

Amy looked back at Adrian. He was writing in his notebook, with his other arm circling the page so that no one could see what he wrote.

Amy got up. "I'll see you later, Adrian," she said. She didn't expect any response, and none came. She walked to the cafeteria food line with Tasha.

"What was that all about?" Tasha wanted to know. "You two were actually exchanging words."

"I was asking him about this clinic he goes to. He won't tell me what goes on there." They picked up their lunch trays and went to their seats. Amy continued to ponder her conversation.

"Tasha . . . Adrian's fancy house bothers me."

"Why?"

"His mother is a waitress and his father is a bank teller. I don't think people make a ton of money in those jobs. How could they afford to buy a house that big?"

Tasha shrugged. "Maybe it's like Eric said. They inherited the house."

"Or they could have paid for the house another way," Amy mused.

"Like how?"

"Maybe they're using Adrian to make money."

"Huh?"

"They might be getting paid by this clinic. Maybe they're forcing Adrian to undergo tests in exchange for money."

"I doubt it," Tasha said. "They seemed like nice enough people to me."

"People aren't always what they seem. This could be part of some horrible plot to examine and analyze child prodigies. Tasha, this could be a huge, terrible conspiracy! Just the way Project Crescent was."

Tasha was skeptical. "Amy, you should take your own advice."

"Which advice was that?"

"Save your imagination for creative writing."

f i 5 v e

The old dream began the same way it used to. Amy was surrounded by glass. She was feeling warmer and warmer. Outside the glass, the red flames were climbing higher and higher . . . but Amy wasn't alarmed, because she knew her mother would be coming to rescue her. At least, that was what had always happened in the past.

But something was different this time. The figure approaching the infant in the incubator wasn't Nancy Candler. It was—it was Amy herself who was coming to the rescue! But then who was in the incubator?

Amy crept closer and peered through the glass. She was staring right into the face of Adrian Peele.

As she woke with a start, Amy's heart thumped rapidly. She lay very still for a moment in an effort to recover from the shock of her dream. Then she sat up and switched on the lamp by her bed.

Now, what was *that* all about? Tasha used to read everything about dreams, and she'd told Amy that all dreams had a meaning. They could reveal something to the dreamer, something the dreamer wasn't able to understand when she was awake.

But Adrian wasn't a clone, that was one thing Amy was sure of. True, he was unusually intelligent, but he wasn't particularly strong. And he bore a distinct physical resemblance to his parents. She felt pretty confident that he was their natural child.

Her hand went to the silver crescent moon that hung from the chain around her neck, the pendant that had the same shape as the mark on her back. Automatically she began to rub it, the way she always did when she was thinking hard. The necklace had been given to her by Dr. Jaleski, the man who had led Project Crescent. Actually, it was Dr. Jaleski's daughter who had presented the pendant to her after her father's death. Mary Jaleski had told her that her father wanted Amy to wear it so she would never forget who she was. So she would remember that she was special, one of twelve, and that none of them would ever be completely safe. In Amy's mind, she'd always felt this meant they should unite someday and help each other.

But maybe the obligation extended beyond the Amys . . . maybe she was meant to help anyone who could be in danger of exploitation, of being used or taken advantage of. That might explain her dream. She had to help Adrian.

The question remained, though—who was putting him in danger? His parents seemed so mild and unassuming, but appearances could be deceiving. Even if they loved Adrian, they might have been tempted by offers of money. And what about the scientists or doctors or whoever was in charge at the clinic—what did they want from Adrian?

Amy clutched the moon pendant tightly. Was it at all possible that the people treating Adrian were somehow connected to the organization that was after *her*? Or were they an entirely different set of evil people?

So many questions . . . enough to give her a headache. Not that she was the kind of normal person who got headaches.

Eric's recent words came back to her: *"You* could get into that study." Despite her mother's joke about Amy's not living up to her potential, what Eric had suggested could work. She could present herself at the clinic, demonstrate her prodigious memory, impress them with the way she could do complex math calculations in her head. Surely that would convince them that she was a genius.

But did she dare go to the clinic? She could be putting herself in serious danger, and that wouldn't do Adrian any good. Not to mention the fact that her mother would *kill* her.

Frustrated and exhausted, she fell back on her bed and slipped immediately into a dreamless sleep.

The next morning, over breakfast, she confided her concerns to her mother. "I have a feeling that Adrian is being tested against his will at that clinic. They could be doing terrible experiments on him to figure out why he's so smart."

"What makes you think that?" her mother asked.

"It's the way Adrian acts. Something has to be bothering him, or he wouldn't be so hostile all the time. And he's very secretive. If his parents are forcing him to go to this clinic, wouldn't that be a form of child abuse?"

"That depends," Nancy said. "For example, a parent can make a child take medicine for an illness, or receive an injection to prevent disease. Even if the child didn't want any treatment, the parent would be acting in the child's best interest."

Amy considered this. "So I'd have to know exactly what was going on at that clinic." She thought she was speaking to herself, but when she saw the suspicious look on her mother's face, she knew she'd spoken out loud.

"Don't even *think* about it."

Amy attempted a look of pure innocence. "Think about what?"

"Going to that clinic and presenting yourself as a genius so you can find out what's happening to Adrian. Amy, we've discussed this over and over again. You are *not* to call attention to yourself."

"I know. I know," Amy replied.

"Amy! Look me in the eyes and promise me you will not volunteer yourself as a subject. *Promise* me."

Amy sighed. "Okay, I promise."

She explained her dilemma to Tasha and Eric on the way to school. "I know I don't always do what my mother tells me to do," she admitted. "But I can't come right out and break a promise."

"I have a solution," Tasha said. "Get someone else to go for you."

"Someone like who?"

"Me," Tasha proposed.

Eric made a snorting sound. "Just because you're good at Scrabble doesn't make you a genius. Besides, if this clinic is doing something unethical, you could be getting into more than you can handle. I say you need to get a guy to go there."

Amy raised her eyebrows. "Excuse me?"

Eric amended that. "Okay, a guy, or a girl who happens to be a clone. Not an ordinary girl like Tasha."

"Thanks a lot," Tasha retorted.

Amy looked at Eric. "Are you saying *you* want to go to the clinic and volunteer?"

"No, not me. I'm talking about Jeremy."

"Jeremy Spitzer? Your tutor?"

"Yeah. I know he's boring and obnoxious, but he's really smart. Adrian told him he wasn't, though, which really pissed him off, so I know he's dying to get into that study. Then he can go up to Adrian and say, 'Nyah, nyah, I'm just as much a genius as you are.'"

Amy seriously doubted Jeremy would ever say something so childish as "nyah, nyah," even to an eight-year-old. And Adrian never would. On the other hand, the kid *did* like cartoons.

But it would help if she could get Adrian to tell her *something* about the clinic before she asked Jeremy to spy for her. She knew Adrian got to school early every morning and spent time in the library's media center. So she explained to Tasha and Eric why she had to dash ahead and began walking at a rate neither of them could match.

The library media center was never particularly crowded before homeroom. Most students arrived later, or spent their time socializing before the bell. The few who were in the library were gathered in a little group, talking quietly.

Except for Adrian, of course. He sat alone, writing in his infamous notebook.

"Hi, Adrian!"

He looked up. Immediately he closed the notebook and stuck it in his briefcase. He didn't respond with a greeting, but at least he acted as if he was waiting for her to state her business with him.

"How's everything going?" she asked.

"Fine," he said.

"Are you making any friends?"

"No. But as I've told you in the past, I'm not interested in friendships."

"Right, right. How about the homework? It's not too hard for you, is it?"

"No."

"Do you like your teachers?"

"They're reasonably intelligent."

She tried to catch him off guard. "What about the clinic?"

His expression didn't change. "The clinic?"

"Yes, that clinic you go to. The one for gifted children."

"Highly gifted children," he corrected her.

"Yeah, that one. Does that take up a lot of your time?"

"Yes."

"What goes on there, anyway?"

"You could visit and find out for yourself."

His response caught *her* off guard.

"I could?"

"Yes. You could be in the study too. Excuse me, I don't want to be late for homeroom." He picked up his briefcase and marched out of the library.

Amy remained standing, trying to absorb what he'd just said. Had he actually told her she'd be welcome to investigate the clinic? Was he suggesting that he *wanted* her to help him? For a second she felt elated. Then she remembered her promise to her mother.

"This is *so* annoying," she complained to Tasha at lunch that afternoon. "He *invited* me to come there. I wouldn't even have to sneak behind his back. It would be so easy for me to just go and volunteer to be a subject."

"But you promised your mother you wouldn't," Tasha reminded her.

"I know."

"That's why you should let me go in your place. I'm not claiming to be a genius, but I'm sure I could impress a doctor with the way I talk. I could manage to hang out long enough to get some real information."

Amy shook her head. "Thanks, Tasha, but I agree with Eric. This could be dangerous."

"I can handle a little danger," Tasha said, bristling. "Just remember who rescued who at Wilderness Adventure."

It was true that Tasha had managed to get away from the evil camp counselor. And she'd located a helicopter and a pilot and got them to come back and take the other campers away to safety. But that had been an unusual situation. Tasha wasn't ordinarily quite so bold.

"No, I'm going to ask Jeremy."

Tasha was clearly annoyed. She stabbed her fork into the brown stuff with little white things and actually ate it. But Amy couldn't worry about her. She'd get over it.

She scanned the cafeteria and saw Jeremy sitting alone. She couldn't go over and talk to him, though. It was an unwritten law at Parkside that boys and girls didn't interact in the cafeteria. There were people who had looked at her very oddly when she'd sat with Adrian the other day. She couldn't risk embarrassing Jeremy.

Yes, he was the best possible candidate to act as her eyes and ears. For the rest of the afternoon, between classes, she was on the lookout for him. She was finally able to corner him right before the last class period.

"Jeremy, I need to talk to you."

He had something besides intellect in common with Adrian. He was just as rude. "What do you want?"

There were only a few minutes before the next bell, so Amy got right to the point. "Would you like to go to Adrian's clinic?"

Jeremy looked pained. "It's not *Adrian's* clinic. It's the Clinic for the Study of Highly Gifted Children. Many others besides Adrian are studied there."

"Yeah, whatever. Are you interested in volunteering for the study he's in?"

"I'm considering the possibility," Jeremy replied. "I haven't decided."

Now was the time for a little flattery. "I'll bet the staff would be thrilled to meet someone like you," she gushed. "Everyone knows you're a true genius, not a freak of nature like some people we know. Eric says you're the smartest person he's ever come across."

She thought she saw a smile, although it was more

like a smirk. "In all the standardized tests, I score in the top percentile," he informed her.

So did Amy, but she acted like this was something truly amazing. "Wow! Then you should definitely go to the clinic."

"Yes, I think I will."

"When?"

He was taken aback by the directness of the question. "Well, I'm not sure."

"How about this afternoon?" She faked a little embarrassment. "I don't mean to sound pushy, it's just that I'm absolutely fascinated with people who are so superior. I'm dying to know what goes on there."

He frowned. "You're not going to volunteer as well, are you?"

"Oh no, nothing like that," Amy quickly assured him. "I wouldn't have a chance. They'd never accept someone as ordinary as I am. But it would mean a lot if you could call me when you get home from the clinic. Or maybe we could get together tonight and talk."

Something very close to fear crossed Jeremy's face. He stepped back in alarm. "I'm busy this evening," he said stiffly.

"Well, tomorrow, then."

"I'm busy tomorrow, too. I hope you won't take offense, but you are really not my type at all."

Amy struggled not to laugh as she realized what was going through his head. Mr. Genius thought she was coming on to him!

Then something occurred to her. With this attitude, he wasn't going to be much of a spy for her.

"Do you know where the clinic is located?" Jeremy asked.

"Yes, it's—" She stopped. "I'll take you there." She hurried on before he could object. "I really want to see the place myself. And maybe I can help you. Vouch for you and stuff. I could tell the doctor or whoever you meet that everyone at Parkside thinks you're a genius."

"I don't think I'll need your help to prove that," he said.

"Well, it couldn't hurt," she said. "What if there're a lot of people waiting to volunteer? They might not have time to test everyone. I'll bet if I make a big fuss about how brilliant you are, they'll take you ahead of the others. I'm very good a making fusses."

She could tell from his expression that she was getting through. "All right," he said reluctantly. "You can come along. Although I doubt that any doctor would be interested in the opinion of an ordinary seventh-grader."

Amy kept her smile fixed on her face until he turned away. Inwardly she fumed. So Jeremy Spitzer thought she was ordinary. Sometimes it was a real pain to keep her secret to herself.

As she waited for Jeremy after school, a tremor of guilt went through her. "I don't think I'm really breaking my promise," she rationalized to Eric. "I only promised I wouldn't volunteer, and I won't. I didn't promise not to go the the clinic."

Eric frowned as he considered her argument. "Your mom is still not going to approve, Amy."

He was right and she knew it. But she'd done a lot of things her mother didn't know about and wouldn't approve of. This was just one more thing to add to the long and growing list.

Jeremy appeared and looked askance at Eric. "You're not going too, are you?"

"No," Eric said. "But take care of my girlfriend, okay? Call me when you get home, Amy."

Jeremy apparently didn't take Eric's words to heart. He walked several steps ahead of Amy as they went to the bus stop. It was obvious to Amy that he didn't want any classmates to see them together. What a jerk.

But she needed this particular jerk, so she bit her tongue.

They got off the bus at Cloverdale Road. Jeremy was watching her expectantly, and she realized she didn't have the address. But she pretended to know what she was doing and started up the street. Her superior eye-sight came to her aid. Way in advance she was able to spot the small sign that read CLINIC FOR THE STUDY OF HIGHLY GIFTED CHILDREN on a door wedged between the Body and Soul Fitness Center and Harry's Discount Shoes.

"It's just up this hill," she told Jeremy. "Follow me." She couldn't resist being in the lead for once.

There was nothing ominous or threatening in the appearance of the clinic. When they went through the door, they saw an ordinary reception room. Everything looked clean and new. There were two low, modern sofas, a table that held magazines, and a large desk, where a young woman sat at a computer. On the wall behind the desk, anchored at the ceiling, was a small security camera in whose lens Amy could see herself and Jeremy. The woman smiled pleasantly at them. "Good afternoon, may I help you?" According to the nameplate on her desk, she was Ms. Merchant.

Amy stepped aside and let Jeremy speak. "I am interested in becoming a subject for your study," he said.

"We have many studies going on here," Ms. Merchant told him. "Are you interested in a particular one?"

Jeremy hesitated, so Amy piped up. "The one that Adrian Peele is in."

She noted a slight change in the secretary's expression. "I see." To Jeremy she said, "I assume that Adrian Peele recommended you to the clinic?"

"Well, no, not—not exactly," Jeremy stammered.

The secretary rose. "Please, have a seat." She left her desk, walked down the hallway behind her, and knocked lightly on the nearest door. Then she went in. The door bore the label A. EINSTEIN, M.D., PH.D.

"Maybe I needed to make an appointment," Jeremy said.

"Yeah, maybe." It was going to be a bummer if no one would even see him today.

But the secretary was perfectly friendly when she came back out. "Dr. Einstein will be happy to see you, Jeremy. You can leave your jacket on the coatrack."

Something about what she said bothered Amy, or maybe it was the way she said it. But Amy couldn't put her finger on why.

Now the secretary was looking at her with interest. "Would you like to volunteer also?"

"No, thank you," Amy said. "I'm totally ordinary. Not like Adrian or Jeremy."

The woman sat down and began typing on the computer.

"Ms. Merchant," Amy said impulsively. "May I ask you a question?"

The secretary looked up and nodded.

"Do people get paid for being in a study?"

"No, they're all volunteers." Ms. Merchant smiled slightly. "There's no salary. If that's why your friend is offering to be in a study, I'm afraid he'll be disappointed."

"No, that's not his reason," Amy murmured. "I was just curious." So that eliminated a motive for Adrian's parents to force him into testing.

"Do you know Adrian Peele?" Amy continued.

"Of course."

"I guess he comes here a lot, huh?"

"Yes, he does."

"He's really smart, isn't he?"

"Yes, he is."

This was getting her nowhere. In desperation, she plunged in. "What does he do here? Take tests? Get checkups?"

The secretary's smile was getting tight. "The work of the clinic is strictly confidential. Now, I have things to do."

The main door opened and a teenage girl came in. "Hello, Kimberly," Ms. Merchant said. "You're early for your appointment. Dr. Einstein is with a client at the moment. Have a seat."

"Okay," the girl said cheerfully. She plopped down on the sofa near Amy.

Ms. Merchant looked at the clock on the wall. "Oh, my, I had no idea it was so late. I have to dash to the post office before it closes." She picked up a package from the desk. "Girls, I'll be away for about five minutes. Kimberly, could you answer the phone if it rings?"

"Sure," Kimberly said. She chose a fashion magazine from the table and opened it. Amy took the opportunity to look her over.

She guessed that Kimberly had to be around sixteen or seventeen. Her tight jeans and T-shirt displayed a perfect figure, not thin or fat, just right. Her hair was an unusually bright golden blond, and Amy couldn't see any roots to indicate that it had been dyed that color.

Kimberly's eyes were large and an amazingly clear blue. Once again, Amy used her super-vision. No, Kimberly wasn't wearing colored contact lenses.

Everything about Kimberly—her nose, her mouth, her chin, and her ears—was perfectly proportioned. She could have been a plastic doll. Amy knew that many people would consider Kimberly beautiful. She certainly represented the standard you saw in beauty pageants.

Amy used to wish that her superior genetic structure had given her that kind of beauty. Now she realized she was better off with her own appearance. Who wanted to look like a plastic doll?

Then Kimberly spoke. "Don't you just hate it when magazines use big words that you can't understand?" She closed the magazine and tossed it back on the table. Turning to Amy, she asked, "Are you in the study?"

"No, I'm just waiting for a friend," Amy replied. "Have you been coming here a long time? Do you know Adrian Peele?"

"No," Kimberly said. "This is just my second appointment. It's so exciting! My parents are totally thrilled. Dr. Einstein says people like me can change the future of the universe! Isn't that cool?"

"Yeah, very cool," Amy echoed, totally bewildered. "Exactly how are you going to change the future of the universe?"

Kimberly giggled. "I don't know. You'll have to ask Dr. Einstein that."

Amy wished she could. "I guess you have to take lots of tests, huh?"

Kimberly's face went blank. "Tests?"

"To show how smart you are."

"No way!" Kimberly laughed. She leaned toward Amy and lowered her voice, as if she was about to confess a deep, dark secret. "I'm not exactly a straight-A student."

Nothing was making any sense. "Then how come you're in the study?" Amy asked her.

"Brains aren't everything," Kimberly informed her solemnly. "That's what Dr. Einstein says. Besides, I happen to be Miss Central Northeast Los Angeles High School. That's how I met Dr. Einstein. He came to the pageant."

Amy couldn't even think of another question. And she didn't have to, because the secretary returned.

"Are you still waiting, Kimberly? Dr. Einstein should be with you shortly."

And he was. Less than ten seconds later, the door of the doctor's office opened and Jeremy came out. Stormed out, actually. Amy was alarmed. Jeremy looked pale, and he was moving with the speed of a convict escaping from a state penitentiary. What had Dr. Einstein done to him?

"Jeremy! Are you okay?"

As Jeremy grabbed his jacket, practically knocking over the coatrack, a man in a white coat appeared at the door. "Thank you for your interest, Jeremy," he said mildly. "Kimberly, you may come in now." As the blond girl scampered to the door, he looked at Amy. "Young lady, are you here to see me?"

"No, I'm not," Amy said as she ran out the front door after Jeremy.

He was already at the bus stop, and the bus was approaching. Checking to make sure no one was watching, Amy broke into a run. She managed to get on the bus just as the doors were closing.

She sat down next to Jeremy. "Jeremy, what happened?"

"It's a scam," Jeremy raged. "That clinic is completely fraudulent."

Amy's heart leaped. Had Jeremy found some evidence for her? "What did that doctor do to you?"

"He made me take a test."

"What kind of test?" Had it involved pain and torture, some kind of physical endurance? Had electrodes been attached to Jeremy's head? Had Dr. Einstein stuck a long, sharp needle into Jeremy's brain?

"It was one of those stupid tests we used to take in elementary school. The kind where you have to use a number-two pencil and fill in the little squares. Questions like 'Plainview is three hundred fifty miles from Springfield. The train travels at seventy-five miles an hour. How long will it take the train to go from Plainview to Springfield?'"

"That's not a very hard question," Amy answered.

"It's simple!" Jeremy said. "All the questions were like that. Another one was 'Which of these words doesn't belong? *Red, blue, green, potato.*' It was the easiest test I've ever taken in my life. I know I must have answered every question correctly."

"So what's the problem?" Amy wanted to know.

"He said I wasn't acceptable!"

"What?"

"That so-called doctor looked at my test and said I had failed! And I'm absolutely positive my score was perfect!"

Nothing was making any sense today. "Are you sure, Jeremy? Because if you answered every question correctly, and your score was perfect, why wouldn't you be accepted in the study?"

"You want to know why?" Jeremy said. "I'll tell you why. It's that little monster Adrian Peele. He told the doctor I wasn't good enough."

"How do you know that? Did the doctor say so?"

"No. It's an intelligent guess."

Amy pondered this. She couldn't buy into Jeremy's explanation. A doctor wouldn't take orders from a patient, or client, or whatever Adrian was called. It was clear to her what had happened. The test had been harder than Jeremy thought. He had failed and now was trying to make up excuses.

But Jeremy clearly believed his own excuse. "If it's

the last thing I do," he muttered, "I'm going to get even with that little brat. There's no way he's going to pull this on Jeremy Spitzer."

It was then that Amy realized what had bothered her earlier, when the secretary had spoken. She had called Jeremy by his name—and Amy couldn't recall his having given it.

It didn't matter, though. Now she had to worry about what Jeremy could possibly do to get even with Adrian.

SIX 6

"**H**e was *so* angry!" Amy reported to Tasha and Eric later that afternoon. Her friends sat at the table in her kitchen while she stirred milk into the chocolate pudding mix over a burner on the stove. "I thought he was going to explode!"

"Really?" Eric's tone was doubtful. "I can't picture Jeremy like that. He never looks happy, he never looks miserable. The guy's a total blank when it comes to emotions."

"Believe me," Amy insisted, turning the dial under the burner. She checked the directions on the pudding box. " 'Bring to a boil, then lower to a simmer.' " She moved the dial to High.

"It must have been a big blow to his ego," Tasha declared. Then she added, "That's his sense of himself."

Amy rolled her eyes. "I know what an ego is, Tasha. I do have some vocabulary, you know."

"He had to have blown the test," Eric decided. "That's why he was so mad."

"But he said it was easy," Amy said. "He even told me some of the questions, and they were really simple. He said he answered them all perfectly."

"Well, he was wrong," Eric said.

Amy looked at the pudding. It hadn't boiled yet. "Jeremy thinks Adrian told the doctor not to let him into the study."

"But why would Adrian do that?" Eric wondered. "What's his . . . oh, what's the word? Lawyers use it."

"Motive," Tasha supplied. "That's the reason why someone does something."

"Yeah," Eric said. "What's Adrian's motive?"

Amy stirred the pudding. "I guess he likes the idea of being the only genius at Parkside Middle School."

"There could be another motive," Tasha said.

"Like what?" Amy asked.

"Maybe Jeremy can't be in the study because he's a human being."

"Ohmigod," Eric said, cracking up. Tasha glared at him. Amy couldn't resist a laugh herself. Tasha refused to give up on the notion that Adrian was some sort of extraterrestrial biological entity.

"Don't laugh!" Tasha yelled.

"Chill out, Tasha," Eric ordered her. "I hate to break it to you, but there are no aliens among us."

"That's not what Fox Mulder says," Tasha said darkly.

"Tasha, *The X-Files* is a television show," Amy said. "It's fiction. That means it's not true."

"I know what fiction means," Tasha snapped. "But sometimes the truth is stranger than fiction."

" 'The truth is out there,' " Eric intoned, quoting the TV show.

This only made Tasha angrier. "I'm telling you, Adrian Peele is just too weird to be real. He's not like other people. Someone that different can't be human."

Now Amy was getting annoyed. "Tasha, *I'm* different. Do you think I'm an alien too?"

"Well, you're not exactly a normal human being," Tasha pointed out.

Eric's eyes darted back and forth nervously between the two girls, and Amy knew why. He didn't know whose side to take. Amy was his girlfriend, and a girlfriend was more important than a sister. But he had to *live* with Tasha.

"Uh, speaking of *The X-Files,* it's almost six," he announced.

A local cable channel was showing reruns of the show every day at six o'clock. Amy had seen most of the shows before, but Tasha liked to watch them over and over again.

"There was another person in the waiting room," Amy told Eric as they moved into the living room. "A teenage girl. She said she was in the study at the clinic. But I talked to her, and I didn't think she was very smart."

"Maybe she's in a different study," Eric suggested. "Was there anything special about her?"

"Well, I guess some people would think she was beautiful," Amy told him.

"Oh yeah? What did she look like?"

Amy glared at him. Why did boys get so excited about the way a girl looked? She'd always thought Eric was above all that. "Let's get back to Jeremy," she said. "I'm worried. He says he's going to get back at Adrian."

Tasha had turned on the TV, and the *X-Files* theme blasted through the room. "Tasha, please turn that down!" Amy yelled. She poked Eric. "Did you hear me? Jeremy said he's going to get even with Adrian."

"How?"

"Well, he's a lot bigger," Amy pointed out.

"Sure, he's older and larger," Eric agreed. "But I can't see Jeremy getting violent. He told me he's a pacifist."

Tasha tore her eyes away from the screen. "That means he's against war."

Tasha's dictionary skills were becoming aggravating. "I know that! I'm not stupid."

"Well, your own mother says you don't live up to your potential," Tasha shot back.

At that moment, the mother she was referring to walked in the front door. "Hi, kids," she said, popping her head into the living room.

Eric and Tasha chorused, "Hello, Mrs. Candler," while Amy murmured, "Hi, Mom." Nancy Candler disappeared into the kitchen.

"Tasha, could you *please* lower the sound?" Amy demanded.

But Nancy's voice was loud enough to be heard clearly over the show. "Amy!" she screamed.

Amy jumped up. "What?"

Her mother came into the room, holding a saucepan. Smoke was coming out of it. "What are you cooking?"

Amy cringed. She'd completely forgotten about the pudding. "Oh, no. I'm sorry."

"You should be. You've ruined this pan! And you could have burned the house down! Amy, this was very, very careless behavior!"

"Maybe we'd better go," Eric said to his sister. "See you later, Amy." They left in a hurry.

Amy couldn't believe her mother had embarrassed her in front of her friends. "I *said* I was *sorry*," she declared. She left the living room and marched up the stairs to her bedroom. She was *pissed*. At Tasha for implying that she wasn't human. At Eric for not standing up for her. At her mother for humiliating her.

And she was still wondering what Jeremy could possibly do to hurt Adrian.

Her mood wasn't vastly improved the next morning. Nancy was setting the breakfast table when she walked in.

"I'm not hungry," Amy announced. "I'm leaving for school right away."

"Aren't you going to wait for Tasha and Eric?" her mother asked.

"No, I've got something to do. When they come by, tell them I went on ahead, okay?"

Nancy looked at her curiously, but Amy didn't explain that she wasn't feeling kindly toward her best friend or her boyfriend. Nor did she want to tell her mother that she needed to find Adrian Peele and warn him about Jeremy.

She was one of the first students in the school building, and her footsteps echoed as she made her way to the library media center. She had just reached the door when Jeremy emerged from inside.

"Hi, Jeremy," she said, but Jeremy brushed past her without speaking. There was an odd, satisfied expression on his face.

Amy gasped. Had he already taken his revenge on Adrian? Right in front of the librarian?

But no, Adrian was sitting at a table, safe and sound. And for once, he wasn't writing in his notebook. He was reading another one of his big fat books.

"Hi, Adrian."

He glanced up. "You went to my clinic yesterday," he said.

She grinned. It was cute, the way he said "my" clinic, like it was his and his alone. "Yes, I did."

"Why didn't you apply to be a subject in the study?"

"Oh, I wouldn't have been accepted," she said. "Jeremy Spitzer is very smart, smarter than I am, and they turned him down."

"Jeremy is not special," Adrian said.

Amy sat at the table and smiled at him warmly. "Do you think *I'm* special?"

Adrian didn't return the smile. "You're unusually strong for your age and size," he said. "Brains aren't everything, you know."

Funny, Amy thought, that was exactly what Kimberly the beauty queen had said.

"I want to find the boy who played the violin at the talent show," Adrian said. He reached down to his briefcase on the floor. "I wrote his name in my—my notebook!" He riffled through the contents of his briefcase. "It's gone!" Real panic appeared on his face, and he jumped up. "Maybe I left it in my locker," he said. Scooping his belongings into his arms, he ran out of the media center.

But Adrian hadn't left his notebook in his locker. It was several periods later when Amy learned what had happened to the precious notebook.

The intercom went on during third period. This wasn't usual. The principal made announcements during homeroom and used it later in the day only for special situations, emergencies, and fire drills.

And it wasn't the principal's voice that came through the loudspeaker. Amy recognized the high-pitched voice of Alan Greenfield, notorious seventh-grade clown.

"I have a special report to make," Alan declared. "We

all know our famous classmate Adrian Peele, the genius. But what does Adrian think of us? It turns out that he's scribbled down his opinions of his classmates in his famous little notebook, and I'm delighted to share some of his thoughts with you."

Amy's third-period teacher looked at the intercom in confusion, and the class went completely quiet as Alan began to read aloud.

" 'Spencer Campbell has a reputation for being a great athlete. This is due only to the fact that he's slightly more powerful than the average puny, pathetic athlete at Parkside.

" 'Claire Marcus is this year's homecoming queen. However, she is merely attractive, not beautiful.

" 'Ninth-grader Steve Runyon has some mathematical talent. He can add two plus two.

" 'Rob Paris, eighth-grade class president, has no leadership skills.

" 'Karen Hale, seventh-grade class secretary, is dyslexic. This is no secret. It's hard to believe the students would elect someone who has difficulty reading to be the class secretary. Clearly, *they* are not intelligent.

" 'Marcy Pringle sings in the school chorus. She has a wide range.

" 'Alan Faulkner, eighth grade. Nothing special.

" 'Delores O'Rourke, ninth grade. Nothing special.

" 'Amy Candler, seventh grade. Unusual physical strength.

" 'Eric Morgan, ninth grade. Nothing special.

" 'Tasha Morgan, seventh grade. Nothing special. Thinks she's smarter than she is.' "

At that point, the intercom went dead. School officials had no doubt switched it off. But the damage was done.

Everyone was talking, fuming, raging, about the young prodigy.

"Who does he think he is?"

"I'm gonna pound him!"

"He doesn't belong here!"

It wasn't hard for Amy to figure out what had happened. Jeremy had managed to steal the notebook from Adrian's briefcase. He'd turned it over to Alan Greenfield. And Alan never passed up a chance to get the whole school in an uproar.

Amy asked permission to use the bathroom and ran directly to the principal's office. "What's Adrian Peele's next class?" she asked the secretary.

The secretary shook her head. "It won't do you any good to know that, Amy. I just saw him, running out of the school. We tried to stop him, but he was too far ahead of us."

Amy closed her eyes. This was just what happened in *Harriet the Spy*.

"I'm going to look for him," she told the secretary. "Ask Dr. Noble if I can be excused, okay?"

And without waiting for permission, she tore out of the office and out of the building.

She ran all the way to Adrian's house. For once she didn't even worry if people saw her racing at the speed of light.

A very upset Mrs. Peele opened the door. "Oh, Amy! The school just called. We don't know what to do! Adrian's disappeared!"

se7en

asha hoped her face wasn't blazing. Fortunately,
her third-period teacher was pretty strict, and once
the intercom had been turned off, she let the students
know in no uncertain terms that there would be no discussion of the incident. And of course, laughter and
teasing would not be tolerated.

But Tasha knew they were all looking at her and no
doubt laughing silently. Others had been identified
in the broadcast as "nothing special"—but she was
the only one in this particular room. She wished she
could disappear. To hear her own name blasted over
the school intercom for everyone to hear was awful.

Never before had she been subjected to such a public humiliation.

When the bell rang, she prepared herself for an onslaught of ridicule. But within seconds of stepping out into the hallway buzz, she realized that she had nothing to worry about. No one was going to make fun of her. People were so united in their anger at Adrian that they had nothing but sympathy for the kids who had been mentioned in his journal. Then she remembered how Amy's mother had compared Adrian to Harriet the Spy. Tasha hadn't agreed, but the same thing that was happening now had happened in the book. When Harriet's journal was discovered and publicized, no one laughed at the kids who had been spied on. Instead, they all turned against Harriet.

And it looked like real life was going to follow fiction. So Amy was right. As usual.

It was lunchtime now. Tasha made her way to the cafeteria and wondered if Adrian would have the guts to show his face. Cafeteria monitors would be obligated to break up any attacks on him, but there was a good chance they wouldn't see the attacks before Adrian had received a few good pokes, or at least a couple of cartons of milk poured onto his little head.

In the cafeteria, her eyes went directly to the table at

the back of the room. It was empty, and she wasn't surprised. If Adrian was a real genius, he'd have to be smart enough to know this was a time to disappear. He was probably cowering in the principal's office at this very moment.

She got on line for food. In front of her were a couple of ninth-grade boys, Spence Campbell and a guy she didn't know. She remembered that Spence had been one of the people ridiculed in the notebook.

The other boy was making Spence an offer. "So how about it? We get the whole basketball team together and we gang up on him."

"We can't do that," Spence said. "He's just a little kid."

"I'm not saying we have to hurt him," the other boy replied. "Just scare the living daylights out of him."

"Nah, there's no point. The kid's history. I heard he took off the minute the intercom came on. He's probably home crying to his mommy right now, and I'll betcha they'll be shipping him off to private school tomorrow."

What had Harriet the Spy done when she was exposed? Tasha wondered. She couldn't recall. She looked around for Amy but didn't see her anywhere. She wondered if her best friend would be as willing to defend

Adrian after learning he'd kept a nasty notebook about them all. Just because he was different, that didn't entitle him to behave like a monster. Just because he was supposedly better than anyone else, that didn't give him license to do anything he wanted.

But that was probably why Amy identified with him. She stopped short, shocked by her own thoughts.

"Milk or juice?" the cafeteria lady behind the counter asked, and from her tone Tasha knew that this had to be at least the second time she'd asked the question.

"Juice," Tasha said automatically. She accepted the carton, paid the cashier, and moved out into the seating area. Then she walked over to her regular table. Tasha was glad to be alone. She had to think through some stuff.

In a way, she was ashamed to have been thinking about Amy that way. It wasn't Amy's fault that she was better than everyone else. She hadn't asked to be created out of superior chromosomes. It was just that sometimes, once in a while, Tasha wished she could do something better than her best friend.

Even that creep Adrian hadn't called Amy Candler "nothing special." Amy wasn't just stronger than Tasha, she was braver and more self-confident than anyone Tasha had ever known. Sure, Tasha had rescued their group at Wilderness Adventure, but she'd gotten help. Amy probably could have rescued them all single-handedly.

Tasha could say she was better at Scrabble than Amy, that she had a larger vocabulary—but even that was a joke. All Amy had to do was read a dictionary and she'd know every word in the English language.

Amy wasn't only superior, she was always right. When the girls had become involved with Melissa Mitchell, Tasha had been in awe of the popular ninth-grader. Amy had had doubts about the girl. Amy had been right.

At Wilderness Adventure, Tasha had had a major crush on their counselor. Amy had thought he was creepy. Again—Amy had been right.

Tasha thought Adrian was an alien from another planet, sent to Earth to examine human beings. Amy thought Adrian was an abused child, being taken advantage of by unscrupulous scientists. Tasha wasn't ready to give up her theory, but she had a sinking suspicion Amy might be right in this case too. It wasn't easy having a perfect best friend.

At the table, Tasha examined her lunch. It wasn't bad that day—a grilled cheese sandwich, soggy french fries, an individual ice cream cup. Unfortunately, for once in her life she had very little appetite. And what little she had completely disappeared when Jeanine stopped by her table.

"Amy is in big trouble," Jeanine announced importantly.

Tasha knew it was best to ignore Jeanine, but she couldn't help asking, "Why?"

"She left school without permission. That's ten demerits, you know. Detention for a week." With a very satisfied smile, Jeanine moved on.

Tasha didn't have to be a genius to figure out why Amy had left school. She'd gone after Adrian. That was another quality Amy had. She never gave up.

But when Tasha returned home from school that afternoon, she had to admit Amy looked defeated. She was sitting on the steps leading up to Tasha's front door, her elbows on her knees and her chin in her hands.

"What's going on?" Tasha asked. "Heard you split from school early."

Amy nodded.

"I left my backpack in my locker, and my house key is in it. If I go back to school, I'll end up getting detention today. And I have to find Adrian. He's disappeared."

Tasha rolled her eyes. "Why do you care? He's not your responsibility."

"Well, I'm kind of his only friend now."

Tasha was appalled. "How can you call him a friend after what he said about your own best friend? Not to mention your boyfriend!"

Amy looked down the road. "Where *is* Eric?"

"Basketball practice. He probably doesn't know you left school. I only found out because Jeanine told me." She slumped down on the step next to Amy.

Amy's brow furrowed. "In *Harriet the Spy,* when the kids found Harriet's notebook and read it out loud, she ran away, didn't she?"

Tasha's memory of the book returned. "Not exactly. She left school, but she didn't run away. She went home."

"Oh yeah, that's right," Amy murmured, and Tasha allowed herself a little pat on the back.

"She was furious," Tasha continued, "but she was also ashamed. And scared of what the kids would do to her. I guess that's how Adrian must be feeling, and that's why he left school."

Amy nodded. "But he's not at home. I went there. His mother's very upset. You know what I think?"

"What?"

"I think he didn't go home because he's sick and tired of it all—the clinic, his parents, his life. I think there's something bad happening at that clinic. Maybe

117

his parents don't even know what really goes on." She frowned. "But there's one thing I still can't figure out. The subjects in the studies don't get paid. So what are his parents getting out of this? Why are they forcing him to be part of the study if they don't get any money for it?"

"Money's not the only reason people do things," Tasha pointed out. "Maybe having their kid in an important study makes them feel like big shots."

Amy's frown disappeared. "Hey, that's it!"

"That's what?"

"The girl I met in the waiting room," Amy said excitedly. "She said her parents were thrilled about her being accepted in the study. Something about how she was going to change the future! Tasha, you're brilliant!"

Tasha sat up straighter. "Thank you."

"Now, the question is—where did Adrian go? Where could he be hiding right this minute?"

Tasha, in a surge of self-confidence, said, "I think I know."

Amy looked at her warily. "I hope you're not going to tell me he was beamed back to his own planet."

Personally, Tasha didn't think that was such a bad suggestion. But it didn't happen to be what she was thinking. "I'll bet he's on the fire escape behind the library," she said.

Once again she'd managed to impress her friend. Amy leaped to her feet. "Let's go!"

Feeling quite pleased with herself, Tasha willingly turned back in the direction she'd just come from. She didn't even mind trailing behind as Amy led the way to the library behind Parkside Middle School. For the third time in less than thirty minutes, she'd thought of something before Amy had.

But her pride was short-lived. Adrian wasn't watching cartoons from the third-floor landing of the library fire escape.

Tasha tried to recover Amy's respect. "Okay, I've got another idea. He *was* watching the cartoons. And in the cartoon, the cat was going after the mouse and—no, wait, a whole bunch of cats were going after the mouse. So the mouse ran away to hide from the cats. He's not afraid of one cat, but a gang of cats is different. Adrian thinks the kids at school are going to gang up on him, so he's hiding somewhere. He identifies with the mouse. Like I told you, these cartoons have a lot of influence on little kids."

Amy didn't look convinced. Tasha tried again.

"Or maybe . . . maybe the cat kidnapped the mouse, and—"

"Tasha, that's it!"

"What?"

"That makes sense! He's kidnapped Adrian! Tasha, you're great! Wait here, I have to make a phone call." Amy ran around to the front door of the library.

Tasha stared after her and tried to figure out what was happening in Amy's genetically superior mind. Was it really, truly possible that Tasha had given her the solution to this weird puzzle?

Amy returned, looking enormously triumphant. "Okay, I think we're on to something. I just called Mrs. Peele. I asked her how she would feel if Adrian wanted to drop out of the study. She told me that she and Mr. Peele would never make Adrian participate in anything he didn't like. So, what if Adrian told Dr. Einstein he wasn't going to be in the study anymore? But Dr. Einstein doesn't want to lose his best subject. So he's kidnapped Adrian! He's holding him at the clinic!"

Tasha clapped her hands. "Okay, let's go to the clinic!"

Amy shook her head. "I can't go back there. They've seen me before."

"Then I'll go alone," Tasha said.

Amy continued to shake her head. "Something bad could happen to you. I think we should wait for Eric."

"Amy, Eric is at basketball practice and it'll be at least an hour before he's home," Tasha said, clearly annoyed. "Adrian could be lying on an operating table by then."

Amy shuddered. But she still wasn't ready to accept

Tasha's offer. "This could be a dangerous mission. If that Dr. Einstein kidnapped Adrian, he's not going to let a twelve-year-old girl get in his way. And if you find out something he doesn't want you to know, there's no telling what he could do to you!"

Tasha refused to be put off by Amy's warnings. "Amy, I may not be a clone, with your powers and abilities. But I'm not stupid. Hey, Nancy Drew wasn't a clone. Agents Mulder and Scully aren't clones. They use normal intelligence to get themselves in and out of dangerous situations. And so can I."

Amy gazed at her steadily. "Are you sure about this?"

"Absolutely, positively."

"Okay. Let's go catch the bus."

"I thought you said you couldn't go to the clinic," Tasha reminded her.

"I can't. But no one will know if I'm hiding nearby."

Tasha grinned. She would never admit it, but she felt relieved to know that her stronger, braver friend would be around while she was spying. Sometimes having a perfect best friend could work to your advantage.

Twenty minutes later, they got off the bus at Cloverdale Road.

"There's a shoe store right next to the clinic," Amy said. "I'll tell them I'm looking for special shoes, and I'll try on a million pairs. It's a new building, and I'm sure the walls are paper-thin. If you think you're in any danger, just bang on the wall."

That sounded like a good scheme to Tasha. The walls wouldn't even have to be that thin, with Amy's super-hearing. In front of the building, she gave Amy a thumbs-up sign as Amy went into the shoe store. Then Tasha took a deep breath, squared her shoulders, and marched into the clinic.

It was immediately evident to her that everyone who went to this clinic was in very good health. People were strolling through the place in shorts and tank tops, and they all had great bodies. It took a few moments for Tasha to realize she'd walked into a health club by mistake. She scuttled back outside, relieved that Amy hadn't been a witness to her mistake.

Now she saw the sign that read CLINIC FOR THE STUDY OF HIGHLY GIFTED CHILDREN. She opened that door and went in. She noted the modern furniture, the inner door, the security camera, and the woman behind the desk. Like a good spy, she noted the name on the desk—MS. MERCHANT.

Ms. Merchant smiled at her. "Yes? May I help you?"

On the way, Tasha and Amy had gone over the story she would use. "I'd like to volunteer to be a subject in one of your studies. At school, my teachers say I'm very intelligent." That much was true, but she didn't think it was very enticing, so she embellished it with a little white lie. "Actually, some of my teachers call me a genius."

"Really? How interesting. Have a seat. Dr. Einstein is with some clients right now, and there's another client coming in soon, but perhaps he can squeeze you in."

"Thank you," Tasha said. She sat down on the low sofa, picked up a magazine, and pretended to be engrossed in it. Her thoughts, however, were definitely elsewhere. Was Adrian Peele with Dr. Einstein at that very moment? What would it feel like to participate in the rescue of someone she didn't even like? And exactly how dangerous was this going to be? She edged along the sofa until she was as close as possible to the wall the clinic shared with the shoe store.

She looked up when an office door opened. The man in the white coat—Dr. Einstein, she presumed—looked rather ordinary. So did the man and woman he was showing out. They looked very happy.

"Thank you so much, Dr. Einstein," the woman said. "It's such a relief to know we'll be able to have the baby we want. Blond hair, blue eyes . . ."

"And you won't forget about the athletic skills?" the man asked the doctor anxiously.

"Of course not," Dr. Einstein said.

Tasha tried to make sense of the conversation. A

baby with blond hair, blue eyes . . . was this place an adoption agency too? Then she caught her breath. Had her suspicions been right all along? Was this place a conduit for the placement of alien children?

She considered knocking on the wall right there and then. But she had no real evidence yet. Amy would just tell her that her imagination was running wild—and Tasha would have to agree.

As the couple left the waiting room, Ms. Merchant spoke to the doctor. "Dr. Einstein, this young lady would like to be considered for a study."

The doctor nodded. "All right." He turned to Tasha. "Let me just write up some notes, and then you can come in for some testing."

Tasha gulped. She wasn't crazy about that word *testing*. But she managed to nod and mentally remind herself that the inner office would be against this very same wall.

The doctor disappeared. Seconds later the door of the waiting room opened and a boy came in. He looked about the same age as her brother, but she couldn't compare them beyond that. While Eric was a healthy fourteen-year-old, this boy looked more like a contender in one of those wrestling competitions Eric watched on TV. He was *huge*—not fat, but big, with bulging muscles that stuck out all over his body.

The woman behind the desk seemed to know him. "Hello, Arnold. What are you doing here?"

"I got an appointment with Dr. Finestein."

"That's *Einstein*, Arnold," Ms. Merchant corrected him.

The boy grinned. "Oh yeah, I always get that wrong."

"And your appointment is tomorrow, not today," she added.

"Yeah?" The boy looked puzzled. "This is Wednesday, right?"

"No, Arnold, it's Tuesday."

Arnold frowned and nodded. "Yeah, I always mix those days up." With that, he turned and walked out of the waiting room.

Tasha stared after him. There was no way that guy was one of the clinic's "highly gifted children"—was he?

The doctor came out again. "Come in, young lady," he said.

Tasha got up. She hoped the fact that this man was a doctor wouldn't give him some special insight into the nervousness she was feeling. For all she knew, she was about to be abducted by aliens.

She saw two doors in the hallway. One was labeled DIRECTOR, the other was labeled A. EINSTEIN, M.D., PH.D. The doctor led her into the latter one.

The office didn't look scary at all. There was a desk,

and a chair facing the desk. Obviously Adrian wasn't locked up here.

The doctor motioned for Tasha to sit, and she felt a lot calmer when she realized that the chair was very close to the wall.

The doctor sat behind his desk. "Now, young lady, why do you think you would be an appropriate subject for our study? Have you been recommended by someone?"

"Not exactly," Tasha said. "But I know Adrian Peele. He goes to my school." She watched Dr. Einstein's expression carefully. He didn't appear at all disturbed by the mention of Adrian's name.

"Anyway," she went on, "I know Adrian is a subject here. I mean, that's not a big secret, right?"

The doctor smiled. "Of course not. Should it be?"

"No," Tasha said quickly. "But, you see, I think *I'm* as smart as Adrian. Smarter, even. So I was hoping I could be in the study too."

The doctor opened a drawer in his desk. "Well, let's see how smart you are." He took out a pamphlet. "This is a little test we give all candidates for our study. Do you have a number-two pencil?"

"No, I'm sorry, I don't," Tasha said.

"People never come prepared for this test," Dr. Einstein grumbled. He went back into his drawer and took out a yellow pencil. "You have fifteen minutes," he told Tasha, and left the room.

Tasha was very surprised to be left alone. She took advantage of the opportunity to do what any good spy would do—look in every desk drawer and examine its contents.

Her search produced nothing of great interest. She found stationery with the clinic's name on it. She saw a staple gun, a box of paper clips, pencils, and pens. All ordinary office stuff.

The search took only a few minutes, but she wondered if she'd have enough time left to take the test. She didn't need to worry. It turned out to be the same kind of standardized test Jeremy had said he'd been given, and that she'd taken years ago, in elementary school. The questions were ridiculously simple.

PUPPY IS TO DOG AS KITTEN IS TO: A. BEAR, B. SHARK, C. CAT, D. KNIFE
BOY IS TO MAN AS GIRL IS TO: A. FATHER, B. WOMAN, C. MOSQUITO, D. EMPIRE STATE BUILDING

Tasha breezed through each question, marking off her answers with confidence. She could hardly believe that a test like this was able to prove whether someone was a genius. All she could see it proving was that someone wasn't a complete idiot!

It didn't take her more than five minutes to complete the test, and she knew she'd answered every question correctly. She spent the rest of the time going over it, wondering how anyone over the age of six could answer any of these questions wrong.

She was getting seriously bored when Dr. Einstein finally returned. "Time's up," he announced. He took the test from her. "Now I'll go over your answers and let you know if you qualify for our study."

Tasha remained in her seat while the doctor read the exam. It didn't take him long.

He looked at her with a pitying smile. "I'm sorry," he said. "I'm afraid the test reveals that you're not a suitable candidate for our studies."

Tasha's mouth dropped open. "What?"

"Please don't take it personally." Dr. Einstein rose from his chair. "There are many, many young people who want to be a part of the clinic's studies, and of course we can't take them all. Only the truly exceptional are admitted—hence our name, Clinic for the Study of Highly Gifted Children. You're intelligent, but not outstanding. Not brilliant."

"But—but—" Tasha sputtered.

Dr. Einstein walked to the door and held it open.

"You must not let this little failure have an effect on your self-esteem. Thank you for coming to see us."

"But—but—" Tasha sputtered once more. She was totally bewildered, but she couldn't find the words to object. The doctor guided her back out through the hall and into the waiting room.

Stunned, she stood there for a moment and tried to figure out what had just happened. The secretary gave her a sympathetic smile. Clearly, she'd witnessed this many times before. "I'm sorry," she said.

"It's okay," Tasha said. In a daze, she barely noticed the young couple sitting in the waiting room. She walked out of the building, turned to the left, and went into Harry's Discount Shoes.

Amy was parading in front of a mirror in a pair of outrageously high heels. Open shoe boxes lay all over the floor. "This isn't the right shade of pink," she was telling a very tired-looking salesman. "Don't you have any in a lighter shade?"

"No, we don't," the man said wearily. "Miss, you've tried on every pink shoe in this store."

Amy spotted Tasha. "Well, I don't like any of them," she said quickly. She sat down, took off the shoes, and slipped into her own flats. "Thank you."

The salesman watched in despair as she walked out of the store without making a purchase.

"What happened?" Amy asked. "Tell me every detail!"

So Tasha did. She started with the couple who had thanked Dr. Einstein for the baby they were going to have. She mentioned the boy who didn't know what day it was. She went over the stupid test. She remembered the couple who were waiting on her way out.

The experience still didn't make any sense to Tasha.

But something seemed to be clicking in Amy's head.

"The couple who was with Dr. Einstein," she said. "Did the lady look pregnant to you?"

"No."

"And the dumb guy who came in on the wrong day—was there anything really different about him?"

"Well, yeah. He looked like a big athlete."

"And would you say the test Dr. Einstein gave you wasn't really intended to help him find out if you're a genius?"

"Absolutely!"

"And that's because he already has a genius," Amy murmured. "He doesn't need any more geniuses."

"Huh?"

"Stay here," Amy ordered her. "If I'm not back in fifteen minutes . . ."

"What should I do?" Tasha asked anxiously.

"I don't know! Use your imagination!"

And Amy ran into the clinic.

e8ght

Amy couldn't see the secretary. A man and a woman blocked her view.

"Yes, Dr. Einstein is expecting you," Ms. Merchant was saying. Amy backed up and silently edged out of the office.

It wasn't the time for a confrontation. If she declared her suspicions in front of all these people, she'd sound nuts. And her suspicions were just that—suspicions. She had no evidence.

Debating her options, Amy decided that she couldn't go back into the shoe store—the salesman would throw her out, and she wouldn't blame him after all she'd put him through. That left the health club on the other side of the clinic.

The muscular man just inside the door nodded to her. "Could I see your membership card, please?"

"Um, I'm not a member," Amy said. "I don't want to work out. I—I just want to hang around for a little while."

The man looked puzzled. "You can't just hang around here."

With relief, Amy noted a sign on the wall. "I want that free thirty-minute trial membership."

The man was clearly skeptical, but he couldn't refuse her. He nodded and pointed to the locker room. "You can change in there."

"Oh, I think I'll just wear what I've got on," Amy said, and hurried into the room that shared a wall with the doctor's office. Unfortunately, this happened to be one of the unusual days when she was wearing a skirt instead of pants. No wonder people were looking at her oddly.

She pretended not to notice the stares and went over to an exercise bicycle just by the wall. This was going to be awkward, but she had no choice—if she just stood by the wall, she'd probably draw more attention. So she got on the bike and began to pedal slowly.

The noise the bike made was a problem. Even with

her super-hearing, she had to strain to hear what was happening on the other side of the wall. But by concentrating intently, by focusing her thoughts and ears completely and solely on the sounds in the doctor's office, she was ultimately able to hear the conversation between Dr. Einstein and the couple.

"Then you definitely want a girl," Dr. Einstein was saying. "Fine. Now, about the child's appearance . . ."

The woman spoke. "I've been thinking about that a lot. Is it more expensive to have a blond-haired child?"

"Wait a minute," the man said. "I don't like a very yellow blond. Could it be more like a strawberry blond?"

"That's a little too specific," Dr. Einstein said. "I can guarantee a blonde, but we can't predict the exact shade. What about eyes?"

"Blue," the man said.

"What about height?"

"Petite," the woman said promptly. "Small hands, but long fingers. I want her to be able to play the piano."

"She'll need more than long fingers for that," the man said. "Can you get us musical genes?"

"Definitely," Dr. Einstein replied. "But again, there's no guarantee that she'll play the piano. She might be more interested in the violin."

"I can live with that," the woman said. "Can we talk about her personality?"

"Of course. I presume you want a child who's cheerful."

"Absolutely," she replied. "I don't want a whiny, cranky baby waking me up at night. But I do want her to be assertive in nature."

"Not too aggressive, though," the man added. "Independent, but obedient."

"And very bright?" Dr. Einstein asked.

"Oh yes," the man said. "But not a genius. I don't want her to be smarter than me. Just above average will be fine."

"One more thing," the woman said. "Can she have a deep voice? I detest high-pitched, squeaky voices."

"We *have* been able to identify the gene that determines tone of voice," Dr. Einstein told her. "I can tape some samples from our subjects and you can choose one. Any more questions?"

"She'll be healthy, right?" the man asked. "I don't want to be facing any big medical bills over the next eighteen years. I'm paying enough for this kid as it is. You folks are charging an arm and a leg for this procedure."

"Well, when you consider that you're going to be choosing the exact arms and legs that you want this baby to have, it really isn't that expensive. We do guarantee a healthy child, though if you want an athlete, that will cost more. Remember, this child isn't going to be cloned from just one source. DNA material will be gathered from a variety of people who have one or more of the characteristics you want, and this material will be blended to produce a particular genetic structure that will meet your demands. You are creating your own baby, and creation isn't cheap."

Still spinning on her bike, Amy felt sick. It was like Project Crescent, only worse. Babies were being made to order, like pizzas.

It all made sense now. The beauty queen, Miss Whatever—her genes were being used to provide a certain physical appearance. The big guy Tasha had seen was a genetic source for parents who wanted athletes.

And they were using Adrian for brains. She'd been right all along. The poor kid was being used, manipulated, taken advantage of. He was a victim of his own superiority.

She was so upset and furious that it took a moment before she noticed that a crowd had gathered around her. They looked awestruck. It was then that she realized the speed at which she was cycling. She was pumping her legs so fast that the wheels spun in a blur and were shooting sparks.

Quickly she took her feet off the pedals. "Excuse me," she said hastily as she jumped off the bike. Running out of the health club, she could hear somebody saying, "Wow, now that's what I call aerobics."

She burst right into the clinic, almost colliding with the couple who were coming out. Ms. Merchant rose from her desk. "Yes? Oh, it's you. You were here the other day. Have you changed your mind about testing?"

"No," Amy declared. "I've come to take Adrian Peele away."

"I'm sorry, that's not possible," the secretary said.

"Wanna bet?" Amy rushed behind the woman's desk and down the hallway. Dr. Einstein was just coming out of his office.

"Where's Adrian?" Amy demanded.

The doctor was taken aback. "Adrian Peele?"

"Yes, eight-year-old Adrian Peele. Child genius. I know you've got him here somewhere and that you're holding him against his will. That's called kidnapping, Dr. Einstein, or whatever your real name is."

"That's absurd," Dr. Einstein said. "If you're not here to be tested, you must leave immediately."

"I'm not leaving without Adrian," Amy insisted.

The doctor took her by the arm. "Oh yes, you are."

Amy struggled to pull herself away from the doctor's grip. As she did, she saw a figure flash by at the end of the corridor. She didn't need to use her super-vision to recognize him.

"Adrian!" she screamed.

She broke free from Dr. Einstein and ran down the hall. There was no sign of the prodigy. Dr. Einstein caught up with her. "Young lady, you are now trespassing. I'll ask you one more time to leave."

"I'm trying to save a little boy," Amy cried out fiercely. "And to save the world from being populated by blond-haired, blue-eyed athletes who play the piano! Bring me to Adrian, now!"

"I can't do that," Dr. Einstein protested. "I'm not in charge here."

"Then I want to see whoever's in charge," Amy demanded.

"That's not possible. The director is very busy right now." He took Amy's arm again, and this time his grip was tighter. "You're coming with me."

With her superior strength, Amy managed to pull away. And before the doctor could grab her again, she ran toward the door labeled DIRECTOR. She didn't bother to knock.

At first the office seemed empty. There was a desk and a big winged office chair whose back was facing her. Then she heard breathing and realized that someone had to be sitting in the chair.

"I know what's going on here," Amy declared hotly. "I demand to know what you've done with Adrian! You're the director, you're the one responsible if anything's happened to him. You'd better speak to me *now* or I'm calling the police!"

The chair swiveled around.

Amy gasped.

"Adrian!"

n9ine

A my was face to face with the small, brown-haired, brown-eyed eight-year-old boy.

"Adrian," she said again.

The child gazed at her steadily.

"I want—I'm looking for the director," she said.

He continued his steady gaze without speaking. Then, in a sudden and horrible revelation, Amy knew the truth.

"*You're* the director," she whispered.

He nodded. "You're intelligent," he said. "Although I'm much more interested in your unusual physical strength. We've had several requests for strong baby girls, and we don't have a feminine source for the physical strength gene."

She didn't feel particularly strong right at that moment. Her head was spinning, and all she could think about was the fact that the director's feet didn't even reach the floor. "Adrian, what's going on here?" she asked. "What have you gotten involved in?"

"It's really quite marvelous," Adrian mused. "A most wonderful enterprise in which everyone benefits. The subjects who provide the genes are contributing to a better world. Parents can have the children they desire."

"And you can make a lot of money," Amy said.

He nodded. "You saw my home. Do you think my parents could have purchased it on the salaries of a waitress and a bank teller?"

"Do they know what's going on here?" Amy asked.

He gave a short, harsh laugh. "Don't be ridiculous. They don't have the intelligence to understand a complicated procedure like this. I told them I was awarded money when I won an intelligence contest. They're just dumb enough to believe that."

She was floored at the way he spoke about his own parents. But she couldn't worry about that now. What Adrian was *doing* was much more frightening.

Adrian, however, was clearly very proud of his accomplishments. "Can you understand what our work here will achieve, Amy? Can you imagine a future in which people like my parents don't exist? Think of a world in which everyone is intelligent and healthy. A world in which logic is stronger than emotion. Parents rarely ask for logical children, but that's a little something I throw in for free. And the parents are very pleased to have babies who don't cry and fuss incessantly. Think about it, Amy. A world in which emotions don't rule."

Amy understood. "You mean a world of blond-haired, blue-eyed people with your brain."

Adrian almost smiled. "Well, that's a sweeping generalization. Some people actually prefer red hair and green eyes. Although it's true that our future generation will be predominantly blond. That's not my fault, you realize. It's what people ask for. And everyone wants a gifted child. You're looking a little pale, Amy. Would you like to sit down?" He gestured toward a chair that faced the desk.

Amy sank into it. "Adrian, why? It can't be just for the money."

"Of course not," Adrian said. "There are easier ways of achieving wealth. I could easily use my computer skills to divert the holdings of an entire bank into my own personal checking account. No, I'm not doing this simply for money." He hopped off his chair. "Actually, my reasons are selfish. I'm sick of dull, stupid people. People like my parents, my classmates at Parkside. I see that you're reasonably intelligent, but you have no idea what it's like for someone of my intellect to have to deal with the general population. It's so annoying. The average person bores me. They have no value."

"But the average person has a right to live!"

"Oh, I'm not planning to kill them off. The thought did occur to me to develop a poison that could be dissolved in the water system. But then the problem of notifying the people I wanted to spare would arise." He shook his head. "Too much paperwork. No, I think my way is best—a gradual repopulation of the earth with superior people."

"It'll take a very long time," Amy pointed out.

"Not necessarily," Adrian argued. "I believe the superior people who are being born through this clinic will take it upon themselves to help rid the world of lesser beings. Through war, perhaps. Superior people will develop superior methods of warfare. Or starvation. The lesser beings won't be able to get work, you see."

"But this is wrong, Adrian!" Amy pleaded. "You're going against nature!"

Adrian looked at her pityingly. "I'd hoped for a more

rational response from you. But there you go reacting emotionally."

"Of course I'm being emotional!" Amy burst out. "I'm a human being!" And for a fleeting moment, she felt as if this was the truth—that she wasn't the kind of creation Adrian was talking about, but a natural, normally functioning human.

And then she realized that, in many ways, she was. The Project Crescent scientists hadn't attempted to eradicate feelings in the clones they produced. In that way, she was the same as Tasha, as Eric, as every normal person in the world. And *not* in any way like the people who would evolve from Adrian's evil genetic tampering.

Because it *was* evil genetic tampering. And Adrian was an evil person. She could see it in his eyes. And now she understood why Tasha could think he was an alien. He certainly wasn't like any human being she'd ever known.

"I can't let you get away with this, Adrian," she said.

"You can't stop me," he replied. "And you're going to help me. You're going to provide me with your physical strength genes."

"No way!" Amy cried out. She leaped out of the chair and went to the open door. Dr. Einstein and Ms.

Merchant were there, blocking her way. The secretary held up a hypodermic needle.

Amy struggled fiercely, but Dr. Einstein managed to get her still just long enough for Ms. Merchant to poke her with the needle. Amy felt the effects almost immediately. A sluggish, heavy sensation came over her, and she went limp.

Thank goodness her brain was still functioning, even if her body wasn't. The needle contained some kind of tranquilizer, but what the doctor couldn't know was that the drug wouldn't affect her as strongly as it did other people.

For the moment, though, Amy closed her eyes and played dead to allow herself time to think. She heard Adrian give directions as the others let her body drop to the floor.

"We'll want hair samples, and you should cut her fingernails. I'd like some skin scrapings too, and it wouldn't hurt to get a pint of blood."

Keeping her eyes shut, Amy frantically tried to figure out how much strength she had left in her body. Maybe just enough, if she took them by surprise. . . .

She didn't have to find out. Footsteps—the sound of many footsteps—echoed in the hallway. And suddenly other people stampeded into the room.

Amy let one eye open a crack and wondered if the

drug was making her hallucinate. What were Eric and the Parkside Middle School basketball team doing in Adrian's office?

Adrian wanted to know too. "Who gave you permission to barge in here?" he screamed. "Get out! Get out now!"

"Don't worry, we're not going to gang up on you," Eric was saying. "We just want to talk to you and your doctor. You need help, Adrian. I'm your big brother. I'm responsible for you."

Dr. Einstein looked at Eric in bewilderment. "You're Adrian's brother?"

'That's right. I'm . . ." He saw Amy on the floor. "Amy! What's going on?"

Amy could feel her remarkable genes coming through for her. The drug was wearing off. She slowly pulled herself to her feet. "Stop him, Eric! Stop all of them! They're trying to take over the world!"

It wasn't much of an explanation, but she didn't have time to say more. Funny how they all accepted her words at face value. Three of the guys jumped Adrian and pinned him to the floor.

But Dr. Einstein and Ms. Merchant had lost no time in making their escape. They were already down the hall and in another second had shot through the clinic door.

Adrian was screaming and kicking, like a typical kid

throwing a tantrum. "What do we do now?" Eric asked.

Amy considered calling the police, but she wasn't sure how much good that would do. She wasn't even sure if what Adrian had been doing was illegal. So she did the only thing she could think of. She went out into the reception area, picked up the phone, and dialed a number.

"Hello, Mrs. Peele? This is Amy Candler. I'm at the clinic. I found Adrian. Can you come and get him?"

She was just hanging up the phone when the door opened. Amy recognized Eric's biology teacher.

"Mrs. Pearlman! What are you doing here?"

"Adrian Peele gave me this address," the teacher told her. "He said I could get information on improving my baby's chances for having an artistic talent."

Amy sighed. "Mrs. Pearlman . . . why don't you just let your baby be what he wants to be?"

ten 10

"Well, at least we saved Mrs. Pearlman's baby," Amy said. "He could have ended up with Adrian's brain."

It was four days later, a Saturday, and one of those rare Los Angeles days when the sky poured rain and there was absolutely no hope of sun. Amy and Eric were sprawled on the Morgans' living room floor. Eric had the TV remote control in his hand. He'd been channel-surfing for fifteen minutes and hadn't found anything they could agree to watch.

"I wonder how many babies with Adrian's brain are already out there?" Eric mused.

"Or how many are yet to come," Amy said sadly. Because she knew there was no stopping the evil genius.

Her thoughts went back to those final moments in the Clinic for the Study of Highly Gifted Children. Mr. and Mrs. Peele had arrived, and they'd been horrified—not by Adrian's diabolical plans, though. They hadn't believed a word Amy told them.

It didn't help that Adrian had immediately gone into a very eight-year-old style of behavior. "Mommy, Mommy," he cried. "They're picking on me!"

"I told you we should have put him in a private school!" Mrs. Peele had yelled at Mr. Peele. "These public-school children are all hooligans!"

She'd swooped Adrian up in her arms and carried him out of the clinic. But from over her shoulder, Adrian managed to give Amy one last look. A look of pure malevolence.

Wherever he was sent, Adrian was smart enough to set up another clinic. It would be hard for anyone to stop him. And even if someone did, Amy had an awful feeling there would always be another evil genius to take his place.

"I should have figured it out sooner," she told Eric. "All the clues were there. The secretary knew Jeremy and Tasha's names without being told. Probably because Adrian was watching everything through that security camera. He knew I was strong, so that's why the doctor kept asking if I wanted to be tested. And he knew that Tasha and Jeremy didn't have anything he wanted, so he had Dr. Einstein give them fake tests, just to get rid of them."

"Dr. Einstein," Eric said. "What was the deal with him?"

"He had to be a real doctor," Amy admitted. "Just not a very honorable one. I'm sure Adrian was paying him a ton of money. I'm also sure that Einstein wasn't his real name."

"How can you be so sure?" Eric asked.

"Because I saw his full name on the desk in the waiting room when I called Adrian's parents. That *A* stood for *Albert*."

"Albert Einstein," Eric said. "He was the famous genius who discovered the theory of relativity."

"Very good," Amy said approvingly.

Eric grinned. "I got that from Jeremy. He's still a good tutor, even if he's not up to Adrian's standards. So the doctor called himself Albert Einstein, huh?"

"Probably a private joke between him and Adrian," Amy said. "Although I never thought Adrian had much of a sense of humor."

The door opened. A drenched, miserable Tasha sloshed into the room.

"You better not drip all over this carpet," Eric warned her. "Mom just had it cleaned."

Tasha stepped out of her shoes and left them by the door. "I wish someone had told me it was supposed to rain today," she complained. "At least I would have carried an umbrella."

"Are you too dumb to look in the newspaper?" Eric asked.

"No," Tasha said. "And at least I'm smart enough to be able to *read* the newspaper."

"Knock it off, you two," Amy said automatically. "Tasha, how did it go at the *Journal*? What did the editor think of your article?"

Tasha slumped on the floor. "He turned it down."

"You're kidding!" Amy exclaimed. She'd read the article Tasha had written about Adrian and the clinic. It had been her hope that the article might make people aware of the dangers in selective cloning.

"I'm not kidding," Tasha said sadly. "He said it wasn't acceptable."

"Why?" Eric asked. "Didn't they like the way you wrote it?"

"No, he said the style was fine. It was the subject he didn't like. He said it was totally unbelievable."

"Oh, come on," Amy remonstrated. "Newspapers

and magazines are full of articles about cloning and genetic tampering!"

"Yeah, I know," Tasha said. "He knows stuff like that goes on. He just refused to believe that an eight-year-old child could be involved. And I'm no Pulitzer Prize–winning journalist—yet."

Amy sighed in resignation. "I guess you can't blame him. It is one bizarre story."

"I should have stuck to my original theory," Tasha remarked. "People are always ready to believe that there are aliens among us. Except you, Amy."

Amy grinned apologetically. "I'd rather run into an alien than another Adrian. And you were closer to the truth than I was, Tasha. Adrian was more than just different."

"Really?" Delight crossed Tasha's face. "You mean I actually knew something before you did?"

"Of course!" Amy said. "You realize lots of things before I do. You're more sensitive to people than I am. My genes don't make me superior in every area, you know."

"But just about," Tasha said, giving her best friend a hug.

"Am I superior in anything?" Eric asked.

"Of course you are," Amy said.

"We just haven't figured out what it is yet," Tasha added.

He faked a punch in her direction, and she scampered away, squealing. Then she noticed her shoes by the door. "Oh no! My new shoes got ruined in the rain!"

Eric took a look at them. "Just take them to a shoe repair. They can get rid of the spots."

"When did you get new shoes?" Amy asked her.

Tasha grinned. "While you were fighting the evil prodigy genius, I was trying on shoes, remember? And after trying on fifty pairs, I figured I had to buy something from the poor salesman."

"That's another way you're superior to me," Amy said. "You have a bigger heart. I tried on a hundred pairs and didn't buy any."

Eric was still fooling around with the remote control. "Ooh, leave it there," Tasha cried out. "I love him!"

"That guy?" Eric said in dismay. A particular MTV personality was on the screen. "He's an idiot!"

"I know," Tasha said happily. "But he's a funny idiot, and he's cute."

"Yeah, keep him on," Amy urged.

And they all settled back to watch a person who probably wouldn't exist if Adrian Peele had his way.

Don't miss

replica

#8
Mystery Mother

Amy knows that Nancy Candler isn't her birth mother—and that, in fact, no one is. All that matters is that Nancy has raised Amy as her daughter, and Amy loves her. Then a woman shows up who claims to be Amy's biological mother and says Amy is definitely *not* a clone. She's got her own explanation for Amy's special abilities. And she wants Amy back!

Amy doesn't know whom or what to believe.

She's drawn to the fascinating stranger.

She wonders why Nancy can't fill in all the blanks in Amy's past.

She begins to doubt her own identity.

Her instincts tell her to dig deeper for clues to her origins. But the truth could destroy the only family she's ever known.